I WOULD LIKE MY NEW BEST FRIEND TO BE

Friendly

Unusual

Funny

Imaginative (likes books)

Very punctual and not off school being ill a lot
   so I don't have anyone to sit with

Nice to me

Coming soon by Susie Day
Pea's Book of Big Dreams

PEA'S BOOK
of
Best
FRIENDS

  SUSIE DAY

RED FOX

Pea's Book of Best Friends
A RED FOX BOOK 978 1 849 41522 4

First published in Great Britain by Red Fox Books,
an imprint of Random House Children's Publishers UK
A Random House Group Company

This edition published 2012

1 3 5 7 9 10 8 6 4 2

The Random House Group Limited supports The Forest Stewardship Council® (FSC®),
the leading international forest certification organisation. All our titles that are printed on
Greenpeace approved FSC® certified paper carry the FSC® logo. Our paper procurement
policy can be found at www.randomhouse.co.uk/environment.

Set in 13/18pt Baskerville MT by Falcon Oast Graphic Art

Red Fox Books are published by Random House Children's Publishers UK,
61–63 Uxbridge Road, London W5 5SA

www.**kids**at**randomhouse**.co.uk
www.**totallyrandombooks**.co.uk
www.**randomhouse**.co.uk

Addresses for companies within The Random House Group Limited can be found at:
www.randomhouse.co.uk/offices.htm

THE RANDOM HOUSE GROUP Limited Reg. No. 954009

A CIP catalogue record for this book is available from the British Library.

Printed and bound in Great Britain by
CPI Group (UK) Ltd, Croydon, CRO 4YY

For Matthew

CHAPTER

1

GOODBYE

'There,' said Pea, propping up her creation on the mantelpiece. 'Told you I'd have time to finish it.'

She stepped back and considered her handiwork. It was a blue plaque – the sort they put outside houses where famous writers once lived, to make people say 'Oh!' and fall off the pavement. This one was more of a blue plate, really. The writing was in silver marker that was running out. She'd spelled *Author* wrong due to the pressure of the moment – but it would do till there was a real one.

'It's *nice*,' said Clover doubtfully, peering over

the top of Pea's head. 'But why isn't my name on it?'

'Mine isn't either,' said Pea. 'Or Tinkerbell's, though I suppose I could add us. Somewhere.'

'Don't bother with mine,' said Tinkerbell, clicking one end of a pair of handcuffs closed around her tiny wrist. '*I'm* not going anywhere.'

With a click, the other cuff snapped shut around the fat wooden leg of the sofa.

With a gulp, the key disappeared down Wuffly the dog.

It was the day the Llewellyn sisters were to leave the sleepy seaside town of Tenby for their new life in London. So far, it was not going exactly as planned. The electricity had been cut off a day too soon. Tinkerbell's father Clem (who had stayed overnight just to keep an eye on things, as he often did lately) had made a bonfire in the front yard to cook toast over, stuck on the end of a twig, and accidentally set fire to the front door. The removal van had arrived three hours early, and left without warning, taking with it breakfast, their hairbrushes, and all but one of Clover's shoes.

But not, apparently, a pair of handcuffs.

Pea was secretly pleased. Clem had put out the fire before she could dial 999, but now they had an excuse. Perhaps she could locate a kitten for the firefighters to rescue too, while they were in the area. In gratitude, they might offer to take them by fire engine all the way to London, sirens on. That would be the ideal introduction to city life.

City life was something of a mystery to Pea, but she couldn't wait to meet it. She'd made everyone play Monopoly after tea for weeks, for research. London seemed to be mostly about rent and tax, going to jail, and being a top hat. Old Kent Road was brown. According to films, there were also red buses, Victorian pickpockets, and all houses had a view of Big Ben. It was going to be brilliant.

'*Please* tell me you've got a spare key for those cuffs,' said Clem as he chased Wuffly around the ancient blue sofa.

'There's a car coming!' cried Clover, wobbling on one shoe.

Tinkerbell sat on the floorboards, cross-legged, drawing a picture of a mermaid with perfect concentration.

Wuffly made a break for the open door of the flat.

Clem gave chase.

The blue plate toppled off the mantelpiece with a smash.

Pea knelt beside the pieces, and clutched her thumbs tightly in her fists. She'd seen it on a poster in the library. It was supposed to stop you from crying – something about redirecting the electricity inside your brain. It never worked.

'Oh, don't, please don't! We can fix it!' said Clover, who hated anyone getting teary (despite being quite the expert herself), especially on important days. But the glue was in a box on its way to London. So were all the other blue plates.

'Well, we'll make another one when we

arrive. A brand-new one for our brand-new house.'

'But it isn't *for* the new house,' Pea said. The new house hadn't earned a blue plaque yet. It was for *this* house, like a goodbye present. But that was the sort of thing Clover wouldn't understand, like saving the nuttiest square of chocolate for last.

Clover eyed Tinkerbell. 'Don't stress. At this rate, we might never get there.'

Pea looked at the plate jigsaw (wondering half-heartedly if the firefighters might be able to fix it), then looked at Tinkerbell, and sighed. As the eldest, Clover was supposed to be the mean one, really, but she'd never been very good at it.

'You can't stay here, Tink,' Pea said gently, taking her drawing pencil. 'Clem burned all the chairs. And you're too little to be left behind to look after yourself.'

'I'm *seven*, not five,' said Tinkerbell drily, producing a new pencil from her pocket.

'You won't even remember this place once

you see our new house,' said Pea, watching as Tinkerbell gave the mermaid horns and a tail. 'I expect it's more like a palace, really. With turrets, a drawbridge—'

'*Loads* of handsome princes,' said Clover.

'If you like.' Pea suspected Tinkerbell would be more interested in dungeons, but Clover was thirteen, and Pea had read all about hormones and mind-altering lip gloss. She herself intended to stay sensibly eleven for as long as possible.

'She's here!' shouted Clem from the stairs as Wuffly barked a mad fanfare.

Pea ran to join Clover at the first-floor window. With a scrape, and a bit of help with pulling the sofa, Tinkerbell followed. Even Wuffly reappeared, to press her wet nose against the glass.

It was a taxi. Not the usual Tenby sort, with DAVECABS and a phone number stickered to the door, but a proper black London cab with an orange lamp. And climbing out was no ordinary passenger.

It was Mum.

Bree Llewellyn, who had lived for the last four years in this tiny first-floor flat with her three girls, making ends meet while she typed, and typed, and hoped.

But Bree Llewellyn was no more. The birdlike blonde goddess stepping out of that taxi was now better known as Marina Cove – bestselling author of the *Mermaid Girls* books.

They waited for her to wave up at them, but there was a handful of girls on the doorstep, clutching books to be signed.

'She's so good with the fans,' breathed Clover.

Privately, Pea thought Clover sounded a bit daft when she repeated other grown-ups' words like that. But it was true: their mother always gave her readers plenty of attention. They watched her pose for photographs, and write her not-real name in the front of books, and Pea very quietly and privately missed the days when she had belonged just to them. Tinkerbell's mermaid, with

7

the horns and tail, ended up on top of a thickly scribbled furniture bonfire, engulfed in red-pencil flames.

Then there were footsteps on the stairs, dainty and clicky.

There she was in the open doorway, great clouds of blonde hair flowing over her shoulders, long skirt shimmering like silver scales. Marina Cove, the famous writer.

'What *have* you done to our front door?' she said, folding her arms severely across her chest.

And then she was Mum again, and everything was all right.

Pea showed her the bits of blue plate, and felt herself wrapped up in a hug that seemed to put it back together again – all wool and hair, and the perfume-smell of jasmine flowers.

Clover limped over – the one shoe that had been left behind was a clog – and joined in, while Clem explained about the fire, and the chairs, and why no one had brushed their hair. (Not that anyone

8

would've noticed. Clover resembled her mother exactly, including the ability to roll out of bed with hair all twirled and tousled as if it had been arranged that way on purpose. Tinkerbell took after her father, Clem, who was Jamaican by way of Birmingham, so her curls needed rebraiding tightly to her head once a week with a blob of CurlyGurl coconut goop to stop her from going fluffy. Only Pea required a regular morning taming, but on Clover's advice she was learning to describe her bright orange mane as 'Pre-Raphaelite' as opposed to 'ginger frizz'. In any case, it did the job of distracting from her chin, which was of a size people mention.)

'I did try,' said Clem, who was looking quite tired by now, and kept glancing hopefully at his watch.

'Oh, who cares about a few tangles,' said Mum. 'I've been looking forward to today for so long, my darlings, and I'm not going to let a single thing ruin it.'

Pea winced, and reluctantly stepped back so Mum could see Tinkerbell.

But Tinkerbell was sitting on the sofa, quite unhandcuffed, throwing a scrumpled ball of drawing paper for Wuffly to chase.

'There you are, pickle!' said Mum, sweeping her up into a great whirling hug of her own. 'Have you been awful for Daddy? I hope so.'

'Of course I had a spare key,' Tinkerbell hissed, once Mum had let her go and gone off to inspect the oddly naked kitchen. She dropped the key into Clem's hands, reluctantly followed by the cuffs. 'You won't tell, will you?'

Clem shook his head wearily.

It was time to go. Especially for Clem, whose job was showing empty houses to people like Mum who needed new ones, and who was supposed to have been unlocking 8 Harbour Court for a nice young couple from Saundersfoot an hour ago.

'See you soon then, girls,' he said, kissing

Mum's cheek. 'I'll come up to visit, check out your new digs once you're all settled, right?'

Marina lives with her three girls and a dog by the sea – that's what it said on the back page of the *Mermaid Girls* books. Clem hadn't lived with them for three years, and he was technically only Tinkerbell's dad. But he was still Pea's Clem – and Clover's, and always a little bit Mum's. Suddenly it felt quite wrong to be going off to all the exciting tax and jail and pickpockets without him.

'Weekly email with all your news, remember?' he whispered in Pea's ear when it was her turn for a goodbye hug.

'With bullet points,' she whispered back, holding on extra tight.

He thudded down the stairs at speed.

'Will he really come to visit?' asked Tinkerbell.

'Of course! We're moving to London, not Mars,' said Mum, tucking Tinkerbell's chin into the crook of her arm. 'Now come on, before that taxi driver thinks we've changed our minds.'

She hurried them out with their one remaining suitcase before anyone could stop for a last look and feel the tiniest bit sad.

'Goodbye, little flat!' she shouted as she tapped down the stairs.

'Goodbye, shower that never stays hot!' sang Clover.

'Goodbye, mouldy ceiling!' said Pea.

'Goodbye, home,' said Tinkerbell.

And they all piled into the black cab. There was a NO DOGS sign, but the driver (whose name was Alexei, and who greeted them all by name like beloveds) said, 'Don't you worry about that, kitten,' to Mum with a wink, and waited for Wuffly to pile in too.

It had nothing to do with fame, Pea knew; people had always liked doing things for their mum. They got a glazed look in their eyes, and suddenly volunteered to carry her luggage, or let her live on their houseboat in Norway for four months. Clover called it being *Mummified*, and was showing every sign of having inherited the talent. Pea was still waiting for hers to develop.

The taxi was much bigger than an ordinary car, and there were flip-down seats opposite the usual kind, which meant you went backwards. Pea and Tinkerbell bagsied them at once, though they promised to swap on the English side of the Severn Bridge if the others wanted a turn. There was also an enormous wicker hamper taking up most of the space in between.

'Who's hungry?' said Mum, flipping open the lid. There were little cakes, miniature bagels stuffed with smoked salmon and cream cheese and small sprigs of something green and grasslike, and real china plates, buckled neatly into place.

Clover and Tinkerbell sat on their hands. Pea was re-reading *A Little Princess*, and they knew perfectly well that she'd spent half the morning making cheese and onion sandwiches to finish up the leftover bread, just in case they suddenly became poor again on the way to London.

But Pea tucked the clingfilmed parcels out of sight, and helped herself without a word.

The others followed suit.

Alexei had two chocolate éclairs, posted through the money-slot of his hatch.

The journey was long. They made a list of all the London places they would visit: the Tower, the Eye, the tea rooms at the V&A (which, Mum promised, had a mad ceiling and very large cakes). Pea read more of her book. Mum gave Clover a pattern book, with real swatches of fabric and rectangles of wallpaper, for her to pick out what she'd like in her new bedroom. Mum discovered the cheese and onion sandwiches, which she said had been a very sensible idea of Pea's, and ate one to prove it. Tinkerbell fed the rest to Wuffly, until she started making peculiar doggy coughs, and had to have a lie down and a belly-rub.

The motorway turned into a busy ring road, then crowded streets lined with unfamiliar shops:

Food & Wine and Chicken Cottage. It didn't look anything like the Monopoly board.

The taxi swung into a quieter road, past a big green park, and puttered to a halt.

Mum said this was north-west London – Kensal Rise (though Alexei had said they should tell everyone it was Queen's Park, as it sounded 'more nobby').

'So, darlings, do you think I picked us a nice one?' She pointed at the house before them, half hidden by a tree: pebbly walls, a crazy-paving path and a red-brick gatepost.

'It's . . . It's . . . Is it really all ours?' said Clover breathlessly.

'Well, only this side,' said Mum quickly, before Clover could mentally annex next door for her own personal music room. 'It's semi-detached. But yes, this whole half is all ours.'

Pea watched Clover anxiously, for she'd been the most excited of them all, and a whole half was still a half, when it came down to it. But Clover began counting off windows – two on the ground floor, two more on the next, and that was just at the front – and she almost skipped up to the front door, leaving her one clog abandoned on the crazy paving behind her.

Tinkerbell regarded the house with suspicion. Wuffly gave another strange cough, then deposited a small puddle of sick on the pavement.

'Good dog,' said Tinkerbell by way of agreement, then shooed her up the path after Clover.

There weren't any turrets, or a drawbridge, Pea noted. Not much chance of a dungeon. But there was a tiny slanted window set into the roof.

'That's an attic, up there,' said Mum, as if she were looking at the house from inside Pea's head. 'It's a bit poky, but I thought you might like it for your bedroom. If you wanted.'

A bedroom, all to herself. In an attic, where she could pretend to be impoverished if being famous and wealthy got a bit dull. She could write her own books up there. One day, perhaps, there would be a blue plaque on the wall outside for Pea Llewellyn, famous writer.

Pea stepped over the sick, and the clog, and ran up the path.

Flat 2B,
Painter Drive, Tenby
Here lived
MARINA COVE
(also known as Bree Llewellyn)
Autor

CHAPTER 2

THE DREADITOR

The Llewellyn sisters had moved house many times, but they'd never had their very own front door before. This one was raspberry red, with a gold letter box.

And it was swinging open to reveal a girl in a fluffy yellow dressing gown, who already looked quite at home.

She had caramel hair and chocolate eyes, diamonds in her ears, and what was probably a beautiful flashing smile – but at that particular moment her face was too busy being horrified by the gathering on the doorstep.

Pea caught Clover's eye, and knew at once what her sister was thinking. Of course a new house all to themselves was too good to be true. It was going to be bunk beds in one room and queuing for the loo all over again.

Visibly sucking in her disappointment, Clover smiled and extended a hand. 'Very pleased to meet you. I'm Clover, and I think we must be coming to live in your house.'

The girl's mouth remained a perfect O of horror.

'Hello again, Vitória,' said Mum, pushing past Clover to grasp the girl's hand. 'Don't worry about the dressing gown. Are we early? We're probably early. I'm awful with days of the week.'

'Yes. No. Sorry,' breathed the girl, yelping, 'Five minutes, five minutes!' behind her as she fled into the house.

Pea peered, wide-eyed, after her. There was a porch, then a narrow hallway with chequerboard tiles. One carpeted staircase led up to another, both with dark wooden balusters. Beyond, she could see a bright white kitchen, with a door out to a little garden.

'So which bit is ours?' said Clover.

'All of it, you daftie,' said Mum, shooshing them ahead of her. 'Nearly, anyway – Vitória has her own little flatlet off the kitchen, but the rest is all us.'

'Is she going to be like . . . Cook?' said Pea, having visions of picnics with lashings of ginger beer.

'Have we got a *servant*?' said Clover, in a rapturous whisper.

'No!' said Mum, giving her a poke. 'We've got a *helper*. She's from Brazil. She's here to do all the boring bits I hate, like hoovering and telling you off. Hmm – I'd better introduce her to Tinkerbell straight away. Now go and fight over bedrooms like normal children, won't you?'

Pea bolted up the stairs at once, eager to claim her attic. It was perfect: a sloped ceiling with a beam – for scratching out the days of one's imprisonment – and a slanted window in a nook with a high-up shelf that would do for a desk, if she sat on a lot of cushions. (There was also a dead spider on the carpet, its legs curled up around its fat body like a cage, but she hoped that was removable. In the meantime she nudged it under the bed with her toe, so it wouldn't get stepped on.)

Then she hurried down the steep white-painted attic stairs to see what the others had chosen.

She watched Clover dash wide-eyed and barefoot from room to room, standing still with her arms outstretched in the middle of each to see which fitted around her best.

Tinkerbell, meanwhile, sat glumly on the bottom step with Wuffly. It was as if she didn't even care about being the last to pick.

It was awful seeing her look so sad, and Pea suspected she *would* care – at the precise moment that Clover set her heart on one particular room.

She shooed her upstairs, with promises of dead spiders under beds.

There was one big bedroom across the front of the house; a tiny one next to Pea's steep white stairs, with a mysterious nailed-up door with no handle on it behind the bed; and an airy room at the back overlooking the garden.

Clover settled on the airy one, which had disgusting orange wallpaper but was closest to the bathroom – 'for morning queue-avoidance', she explained.

Clover was the only one who made morning queues for the bathroom, since no one else took twenty-five minutes to wash their face. But she looked so happy, Pea didn't mention it.

'Which one are you having, Tink?' Clover asked, twirling her across the landing. 'Suppose Mum ought to get the biggest, really.'

Tinkerbell took one step into the tiny room, and shrugged. 'OK.'

'Are you sure?' asked Pea.

'Of course she's sure!' said Clover, twirling Pea too. 'It's gorgeous. It's *perfect*. This is like my dream house. Can you believe we actually live here?'

Pea couldn't, quite. Even Tinkerbell looked less gloomy, now she'd discovered her tiny room had a mysterious nailed-up door to nowhere – and for a moment Pea wondered if that might be even better than an attic with beams and a dead spider.

It really was the perfect house.

'Oh no!' Mum wailed from downstairs. She had pulled open the door to a yellow room with sunlight pouring through the windows. In the middle of the room was everything they owned, all in cardboard boxes labelled *Pea's Books*, *Living Room*, and so on, in Clover's spirally handwriting.

'I suppose the removal people didn't know which room was which,' said Mum, lifting one labelled *Study* and wandering aimlessly into the hall with it.

Unpacking commenced.

Pea laid out her best notebook with silver

stars on the cover, and her diary, and her favourite pen on her shelf-desk, and wrote a brief poem while standing up entitled 'On Moving House':

We've got a new house, I live in the attic
With sisters, one evil, one melodramatic,
A mum and a dog,
Some sick and a clog,
And a helper who's Braziliatic.*

(*NOT SURE ABOUT THIS – LOOK IT UP)

Clover relocated her two and a half pairs of shoes, and laid them out, with a large empty space beside them for the brand-new ones she would soon own.

Tinkerbell occupied herself with the very careful sorting of the boxes in the sun room.

'I'm being helpful – stop looking so surprised,'

was all she would say as she ferried them one by one up the stairs.

Vitória reappeared, now dressed impeccably in jeans and a pink vest, and began making fierce-looking coffee in miniature cups.

'Mum!' yelled Pea. 'I haven't got any bookshelves!'

'I haven't got a wardrobe!' yelled Clover.

'*Oh,*' said Mum, plonking the box down on a desk she'd forgotten to buy, and sinking into an armchair that didn't exist.

And that was how they discovered that the few bits and pieces of furniture that they had brought from the little flat in Tenby did not fill up the empty spaces in their perfect house in London.

When Pea set up Mum's battered old computer in the study – balanced on a desk of upturned cardboard boxes – there was no internet.

There were no curtains at the windows.

And if Tinkerbell flipped the light switch in her appointed little room, nothing happened – for the

25

people who had lived here before had, it appeared, unscrewed every last light bulb and taken them for their own new house.

They perched in a line along the kitchen countertop, and made a list of the things that were missing. That meant shopping. Clover's eyes lit up, and she took charge of the pen, adding designer suggestions from the pattern book.

'Are you really from Brazil?' Pea asked Vitória, fascinated by the perfectly manicured hand holding the tiny coffee cup.

'Yeah, I'm from Recife,' she said. (It sounded like *Heh-see-fee* when she said it.) 'But I work in UK to improve my English, innit. Been here two years now. I never met nobody called names like you, though. They are kind of . . . peculiar weirdo crazy-people names, yeah?'

'Do you think so?' said Clover.

'We've never noticed before,' said Pea.

'You're totally the first person to ever mention it,' said Tinkerbell.

Mum groaned. 'Excuse my brats. Yes, Vitória, they are unusual names – and not one of them is my fault, so the three of you can stop looking so accusing.'

'My dad chose mine for me,' said Clover.

'A clover is a flower, yeah?'

'A weed,' said Tinkerbell.

'A wild flower,' Clover corrected. 'They're lucky. It means I'll probably be famous too, like Mum.'

'Clover and I got to name Tinkerbell,' said Pea, 'because Mum was all space-cadetty on gas and air in the hospital, and the nurses asked us what our new baby sister was called. We were in a fairy phase at the time.'

'I'm the not-lucky one,' said Tinkerbell.

'You are! We were into dinosaurs a few weeks later. You could've been Stegosaurus Llewellyn.'

'I understand,' said Vitória, who didn't really. 'And you are Pea? This is like a vegetable, yeah?'

There was a small silence while Clover and

Tinkerbell looked at Pea, and Pea looked at the floor. Pea's real name was Prudence – after the song that had been playing in the hospital the moment she was born – and when she was small she used to have a violent lisp. After a tearful first week of school spent introducing herself – to universal confusion – a kind-hearted teacher had intervened, and although they had moved several times since, Pea (and its spelling) had stuck in place of Pwudenthe. It was, however, something of a family secret.

Everyone waited to see if Mum would invite Vitória in on it. But she stroked Pea's overflowing red ponytail, and said brightly, 'Yes, like the vegetable. Why should flowers hog all the attention, after all?'

So that was all right. They were still Mum, three girls and a dog, like before.

Vitória peered at the shopping list. 'I can do Tesco run in a bit. What do you like? We should have special new-home dinner, yeah?'

'Pot Noodle!' said Tinkerbell. Pot Noodle was definitely treat food, since they only ever had it when Clem was in charge, and he always made them bury the slimy plastic leftovers at the bottom of the bin.

'Volcanoes!' said Pea. 'Those are cheese-and-baked-bean toasties, in case they don't have those in Brazil.'

'You can't ask for those,' said Clover, blushing on their behalfs. 'We have to eat posh food now, like caviar and quail's eggs and fish with their heads still on. Our mother is a very famous writer, Vitória, in case you didn't know.'

Mum threw a biro at her head. 'Clover! Famous writers eat cheese-and-baked-bean toasties just like everyone else. Especially when they've got to buy half a houseful of furniture.' She took the list from Clover's hand, and sighed. 'If I bought even half of this stuff we wouldn't be eating anything at all.'

'But the hamper, with the tiny bagels!' protested Clover. 'And the taxi!'

'The hamper was a treat! And the taxi too. I thought it would be fun – but really we only did it because it was cheaper than all four of us going on the train. We might have to be Well-Behaved for a little while.'

Clover stiffened.

Being Well-Behaved meant the grey kind of fish fingers; no chocolate biscuits; late strange tea because Mum was waiting for the reduced things that were about to go off; family-only birthday parties because there was nothing to put in the party bags; too-tight shoes and borrowed coats. It had happened a lot before Tinkerbell was born, but not since Mum had written the *Mermaid Girls* books.

'Plain pasta with hot tinned tomatoes for our new-home dinner, then,' sighed Tinkerbell.

With a sudden erupting sniffle, Clover fled, her sobs keeping time with her feet thudding up the stairs.

'She's not usually like that,' Pea whispered

to Vitória. It wasn't strictly true, but she was worried honesty might make Vitória take her diamond earrings and tiny coffee cups off to a less overwrought family.

Hiccupy crying noises floated down through the kitchen ceiling.

Mum's eyes began to fill with tears too.

'I'll go,' said Pea quickly.

She found Clover in her orange room, weeping over the pattern book of wallpaper swatches.

'I've got eight minutes left!' she wailed, brandishing her alarm clock. Clover's tearful moments could last hours, and at Pea's request (since she was invariably the one who did the soothing), Mum had instigated a ten-minute time limit on all sad cries. It worked surprisingly well.

After three tissues, Clover reached the gaspy but talkative stage, where everyone can see your red nose and burning cheeks, so you might as well say all sorts of things out loud. She said that she wasn't being spoiled, and she didn't mind at all that it was only a whole half a house, and no coathangers, and there being an unexpected Vitória on the front step. But this was supposed to be her perfect dream house, and she wanted nice wallpaper. Not orange. Lilac, with tiny white flowers and splashes of gold.

Pea wasn't a very wallpaper-minded sort of person, but she thought she understood. Mum arrived with a cool flannel for dabbing on puffy eyes.

'Oh, my flower, the pattern book was just for ideas! You can't point your finger at every expensive thing you take a fancy to and expect it to materialize. I'm not made of money.'

'You are! It was in the local paper.'

'Well, the paper is stupid. I've made a nice bit of money, yes, much more than all but a tiny handful of writers ever do – certainly more than we've ever had before – but I used it all up for the deposit on this house, and I still have to pay lots more before we'll own it properly. And now there's Vitória, and I've got to buy boring things like lampshades, and a lawnmower, and one of those fluffy things you put round the bottom of the toilet.'

'So we're poor again? Only in a nicer house?'

Pea thought ruefully of the cheese-and-onion sandwiches.

'No! Not poor. But I might have to write another book before we can buy special wallpaper with gold in. Maybe two.'

Suddenly Mum gasped. Her mouth twisted up like a toffee wrapper, and her cheeks went pale. 'What day is it?' she breathed, clutching Clover's wrist.

'Um. Tuesday. Tuesday the twenty-fourth.'

She grew paler.

'Oh no,' said Pea. She had seen that look before. 'Not the Dreaditor?'

Mum nodded weakly. 'She's coming for lunch on Friday. I promised her a guided tour and ten thousand words. I haven't written a sentence. And we've got nothing to sit on.'

Pea gripped her mum's hands supportively. This was a *true* crisis. They had never met, but Pea knew that Nozomi Handa, the Dreaded Editor, was not the sort to submit to Mummification in the face of undone homework – nor to cheerfully perch on the kitchen counter.

'We'll fix it,' Clover promised, looking plaintively at Pea as if all her wallpapery future depended on it. 'Won't we?'

Pea nodded.

'You go to the study. Tink will feed you paper. We'll do the rest. Just write!'

Clover was sent to the little door off the kitchen marked PRIVATE, to explain it all to Vitória.

Tinkerbell was instructed to put Wuffly in the shed if she went barky.

Pea hunted frantically through all the boxes marked *Kitchen*, and made the Special Writing Tea – a six-sugar cupful.

SPECIAL WRITING TEA
Large spotty WE ♥ MUM mug
1 peppermint tea bag
1 teaspoonful coffee
1 teaspoonful hot chocolate
1–6 sugar cubes (1 for mornings, 2 for a
new chapter, 3 for a chase, 4 for a kiss, 5
for death, 6 for a deadline)
Twix (for stirring)

They sat at the bottom of the stairs, waiting for the telltale *clicky-click* of the keyboard to begin.

Instead, there was a wail.

'The Holy Scriptures!'

The Holy Scriptures were, in the Llewellyn house, a haphazard bundle of notebooks, loose pages and diagrams on the backs of café napkins. They contained the full history of the Mermaid Girls, past, present and future. Each character had their secrets noted down for later use, along with plot ideas and the occasional furtive handwritten scribble: *Is this a bit rubbish?* or *May have stolen this plotline from Buffy the Vampire Slayer: watch all of season 4 again IMMEDIATELY!* If ever Marina Cove's inspirational well ran dry, the Holy Scriptures were there.

Until now.

'I packed them, I really did!' said Pea, rooting through the last boxes in the sun room.

'They were absolutely the first thing we put on the removal van, I remember,' promised Clover.

Tinkerbell pulled her bedroom door closed – quite firmly – and declared that Wuffly urgently needed a walk.

Vitória took them all off, to give Mum some peace. No one was in the mood for being Well-Behaved yet, so they went to the chip shop for tea, and ate their special new-home dinner on a bench outside. Pea had a battered sausage and extra vinegar on her chips. At bedtime, Mum took a long enough break from writing to screw in a few light bulbs before tucking them in with a kiss and a quavery smile.

Pea curled up in her narrow bed, thinking how thrilling it was to be in an attic all of her own – until she remembered the curled-up dead spider, and the unfamiliar house started making unfamiliar creaky noises that sounded like axe murderers on the stairs. The mattress was harder than her old one. The streetlight outside cast odd shadows through the curtains. No matter how many special London sheep she tried to count, sleep would not come. Eventually she crept down the attic stairs in the dark, saw a light still on in the tiny bedroom, and snuggled up at the end of Tinkerbell's bed. Ten minutes later, Clover joined her, mumbling something about 'too much space'.

The following morning they woke in a heap of duvet on the floor. Mum, meanwhile, was found asleep at her cardboard-box desk, a keyboard pattern stamped into her cheek, a blank page waiting under her uncapped pen.

Pea began to panic.

But by Thursday Vitória had roused half the au pairs in London in a second-hand furniture scavenge. She drove Pea at terrifying speed through the city, collecting bits and pieces in her silver open-topped car (not the sort of car Pea expected a not-a-servant to drive, though she couldn't work out a way to ask about it without sounding spectacularly rude), and only slowing down when a borrowed beanbag exploded, scattering white balls of polystyrene all over Primrose Hill.

Back at the house, the doorbell brought a box of *Mermaid Girls* books to be signed, and a small pile of letters from readers, marked *Marinamail! URGENT!* in cross red marker. Pea took them up to her attic, and embarked on a new career in signature forgery. She posted the nicer letters under the study door as encouragement, along with helpful writerly suggestions.

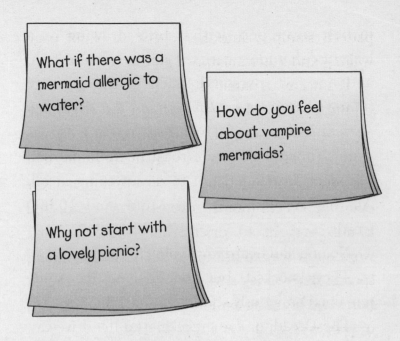

What if there was a mermaid allergic to water?

How do you feel about vampire mermaids?

Why not start with a lovely picnic?

Furious typing resulted.

By Friday lunch time the house was quite convincing. True, the sofa was inflatable and had Hannah Montana's face on it. The armchairs in the sunny yellow room were mismatched and threadbare and came from a skip – but Clover had added bright cushions, and mugfuls of flowers on the windowsills. Pea had signed all the books in best silver pen, with a little drawing of a leaping fish underneath the squiggly autograph, and her own personal touch in the message (*Please tell everyone you have ever met that this is your favourite book – even if it isn't. Yours hopefully, Marina Cove*). Vitória had made roast beef. Tinkerbell had been instructed not to do anything at all. All they needed now was Mum, and 10,000 words.

No one had heard any typing for hours.

They knocked, but the door to the study remained ominously shut.

The Dreaditor came clicking up the driveway. Nozomi Handa of Marchpane Books wore her hair in a perfectly straight black fringe high above her eyebrows. A slash of red lipstick, an expensively stretchy black dress, and purple striped tights completed the ensemble. Pea hoped that anyone trying so hard to look witchy must be secretly nice. But they all remembered that time Mum had thrown the first draft of *Mermaid*

Girls 2 in the sea, howling, 'Nice enough, if a little derivative!' at the sky. Pea knew the feeling well. She felt as if she herself were waiting in her old Tenby Primary classroom, as Mrs Davies handed back their 'Evacuee's Diary' projects; recalled that prickle of shame as hers flopped onto her table marked *C+: Good effort (if a little fanciful!)*

PEA LLEWELLYN, YEAR 6, CREATIVE WRITING

Miranda's diary, 25 December 1941
Tonight we found a German soldier in a barn, and didn't stab him, though we were tempted obviously on account of him being an awful Jerry. But it was Christmas, so we played football instead and offered him some turkey. Then Mr Andrews put him back in the barn for the night, just in case.

41

26 December 1941
When we looked this morning the soldier was gone! I hope he isn't a spy. We gave him plum pudding and everything.

26 December cont'd
He IS a spy! Oh no! They're bombing us now ...
uh ... ow ... *dies*

'Charming little house!' declared the Dreaditor, kissing air instead of cheek as the girls introduced themselves. 'Shabby chic: so fashionable.'

Clover smiled tightly. Vitória brought coffee, and effortless distraction in the form of shoetalk. The Dreaditor sat down on the sofa, which instantly let out a slow whine and began to list to one side.

Pea hammered ever more urgently on the study door. Eventually she gave in and opened it – only to find nothing but screwed-up balls of paper, abandoned teacups, and the window (which was at perfect escape height) wide open.

'Oh no,' said Clover, appearing at her shoulder. 'Where's she gone?'

Tinkerbell's clear, unsupervised voice could be heard from the hall, over the ever-louder whining of the deflating sofa:

'So if Mum hasn't actually written the next bit of book yet, will she have to give you all the money back?'

The Dreaditor gave an alarmingly thin laugh. 'She's a professional, dear – of course she'll have written it. Where is my Marina, anyway?'

Pea stared bleakly at the empty study. It was no use. They'd tried, but the truth would have to come out.

Then the doorbell rang, and on the step was Mum, arms stuffed with papers, and sparkles in her eyes.

'Morning! Thank you, my creatures – thought

I might have to climb back in through the window and I'm not dressed for burgling. Wuffly, get down! I know I've got pastry on my fingers but that doesn't mean you get to chew them. Did you know there's a café in Queen's Park? A nice noisy one, and it does cinnamon twirls and I had *four*, which isn't sensible but they don't last very long, and I've been there since it opened. No sleep at all! Last night a brand-new mermaid popped into my head and wouldn't go away, so I took her for a walk in the dark, and started thinking of things for her to do, and I've been writing and writing. I've got these lovely new pages and a whole new synopsis, and it's just so much better than I thought it would ever get, even yesterday, and— Nozomi, you're here! What *has* happened to that sofa?'

She broke off to give everyone hugs.

'It's so lucky we moved house! I had all these ideas written down in the Holy Scriptures, and when they got lost I thought I might as well just climb into the fridge and refuse to come out till

January, but I'd never have thought of Beryl if I still had them. It's as if losing them let all the good new ideas come out to play. She won't really be called Beryl: that's a terrible name for a mermaid. Can I smell roast beef?'

The Dreaditor and Mum sat together in the flowery armchairs from the skip to have grown-up booktalk. When they emerged, Mum was pink-cheeked and tearful, but still smiling. That meant it had gone *extremely* well.

They all gathered around the kitchen table to eat, Pea feeling strangely nervous on Vitória's behalf. The Dreaditor declared the beef very good in the middle but in need of a little trimming, and the Yorkshire puddings best edited out altogether – but right after she'd said that, the gravy boat dribbled all down her expensively stretchy dress, in a blatant act of revenge.

After three more cups of Vitória's coffee, the Dreaditor clicked off down the drive.

The house fell quiet. Suddenly, after all the

panic, there was nothing very urgent to do.

Mum walked around in a daze, admiring the new old furniture, and phoning all Vitória's friends to say thank you again and again.

Tinkerbell threw leftover Yorkshire puddings around the garden for Wuffly to catch.

Upstairs, Clover contentedly hummed *Somewhere Over the Rainbow* and (with permission, and a pot of Vitória's nail polish) began to paint tiny silver flowers onto her four orange walls.

Pea decided that the poem about the dramatic attic might work better as a short story. Her notebook was not under her pillow (where it generally lived, for easy access in case of night-time inspiration), and it took a small amount of room-destruction before she remembered where it must be: Tinkerbell's room, where she'd curled up to sleep the night before.

It wasn't on the floor, or on the chest of drawers. Guessing it had fallen down the back of the bed, Pea got onto her hands and knees, and peered.

It was dark and dusty, apart from a line of light glowing through from the house next door, underneath the mysterious nailed-up door.

There it was, her best notebook with the silver stars on the cover. Resting on top of a cardboard box labelled *Holy Scriptures: Take Care!!* in scrolly handwriting.

'Spooky,' said Tinkerbell, when confronted. Even Wuffly looked the picture of innocence. '*No* idea how they ended up down there.'

And that was all she would say about it.

CHAPTER 3

A LONDON PEA

For the first few weeks London proved to be a very Llewellyn-ish sort of city. Vitória (who had revealed a knack for exotically twisty hairdos and did not mind sharing her jewellery box, thus earning Clover's undying affection) had worked for a family in Belsize Park before theirs. She knew all the best places to take them.

4 August

Dear Diary,
Today we went to the British Museum. There

are mummies, and rocks, and an old old library filled with old old books, hidden in a huge round white room, like a fruit cake with icing on the outside. Then we went shopping. Tinkerbell got lost in Oxford Circus Topshop.

Vitória has bought me and Clover an Oyster card. You hold it over a yellow circle and it beeps to say you can go on the Tube. Clover says only tourists use ordinary tickets, and it proves you are a real London person if you have one.

I love being a real London person. I have now been to all the green ones on the Monopoly board!

6 August

Dear Diary,
Today we went to Covent Garden. Clover bought soap that is in the shape of a lime but it just smells like soap to me. Tinkerbell got lost

49

on the escalators. We had to ask a lady to make an announcement to the whole Piccadilly Line.

10 August

Dear Diary,

Today we were going to go on the London Eye but it was cloudy so we went to Kilburn Library and then out for pizza instead. I had a Capricciosa. It was crispy. Tinkerbell got lost in the toilets.

Tink says she keeps getting lost because London is too big and full of people.

London is definitely a bit too big. I have now collected all the stations except Fenchurch Street, because Vitória doesn't know where it is. I know where all the places are in Tenby. In Tenby pizza isn't crispy, it is Cheesy Heaven like it says on the sign outside Marco's.

Tinkerbell didn't only get lost. She put salt in the Special Writing Tea instead of sugar, sneaked her red socks into the white washing, and put peanut butter in Vitória's bra. (She denied the last one, and tried to blame Wuffly, but dogs are not good at unscrewing jars.) Pea was shocked. Tinkerbell had always been ever so slightly malevolent – whenever they watched *The Snowman*, she would rock with laughter while everyone else sobbed at the ending – but never in a mean way. When they discovered that Tinkerbell's new handmade ceiling mobile was constructed from Pea's missing gel pens and Clover's beloved *Grease* CD, it was the last straw.

'You're horrible!' shouted Pea.

'You're horribler than I am!' shouted Tinkerbell, slamming her bedroom door.

'I wish we'd left you behind in Tenby!' shouted Clover, slamming her door too.

'So do I!' shouted Pea, wondering if she should run up the attic stairs and slam hers as well. (They hadn't had separate bedroom doors to slam before. It was a whole new way of having an argument.)

'So do I,' said Tinkerbell through the door – not shoutily or cross this time; rather serious and sad.

Pea worried, and went to fetch Mum, but she was already coming upstairs to complain that door-slamming didn't go very well with trying to invent a new kind of mermaid. After some whispered explanations, Mum sent Pea off to join Clover, and went into Tinkerbell's room, closing the door gently behind her.

Ten minutes later, Mum came to sit between them on Clover's bed, wrapping her arms around their shoulders and filling Pea's nose with that warm, woolly, jasmine-flower Mum-smell.

'I know she's been completely Stinkerbell,' said Mum, 'and she will come and say sorry – but I want you two to be very grown-up about it. It's been a big change for her, this move, and—'

'We know. She misses Clem,' Clover said knowledgeably. 'It's really only to be expected.'

Pea thought that this was the sort of sensitive middle-sisterly thing that she should have noticed herself, and felt awful. Clem had come to visit a couple of weeks after they'd moved in, bringing a bucket of Tenby beach sand (Mum's idea) to help them feel at home. He phoned often, and Pea sent him a weekly email (with bullet points), but it wasn't the same as him popping round for tea and a custard cream whenever he was passing.

'*You* like London, don't you, darlings?' said Mum, giving their arms a squeeze.

'Of course!' said Clover, and she looked so beamingly pleased, and Mum looked so relieved, that it seemed wrong for Pea to say anything but 'Yes.'

But Pea missed Clem too. She missed fluffy Tenby pizza. Most of all, Pea missed her best friend, Dot. Dot was small and rabbit-like, giggly and very sweet. They were inseparable, and had

53

made solemn promises to go on sitting together when they went up to Big School in September, which Pea still felt guilty about breaking (not to mention worried about who she herself would sit beside). Clem's bucket of sand – now tipped out on the patio, going crusty in the rain – only reminded her that it was the summer holidays, and Dot must now be messing about on Tenby beach without her.

It was all well and good being a real London person with an Oyster card that beeped, Pea thought, but not if there was no one unLondonish to tell about it later.

Every week she had sent off two or three postcards of Famous London Landmarks, so that Dot would feel at home if she visited. None came back in return. Pea had visions of various tragic fates that could have befallen poor Dot: swept off the beach by sea monsters; kidnapped by square-toed witches; locked in a dungeon, waiting helplessly for her best friend to realize, and rescue her.

When at last an envelope plopped onto the mat addressed to Pea Llewellyn, the relief was enormous. But the letter began:

Dear Pea,

Omigod!!! It has been aaaaages – soz!!!!!! I've been totally mad busy all summer cos of gymnastics (I told you I was starting gymnastics again, right? Well I did anyway), and it is like the best but so busy and tiring and I have had like no time off!!!!

On and on it went, over four typewritten pages.

What we do is we have to get up at 5.45 in the morning (I know!!!!!) and then Nana drives me to Pembroke Dock where the gym is which takes half an hour and then we do stretching and then we do rotation which is like when you go round all the different stations in the gym and do each one for a while and then the next one and then the next one and then we have breakfast. Then we do more stretching and then we do focus which is when you focus on your specialism. My focus is beam though I like floor better because you can do more different things but I am best at beam and Amanda who did beam before fell off and broke her spine so they need a girl to be beam. It's good though because Esme who is my best friend does asymmetric bars and they are next door to beam so we get to play DS together.

At the end it was signed 'Dotty xxx' and there was a photo in the envelope, printed off the computer, of a girl with scraped-back hair wearing a glossy skin-tight white and red leotard. She was standing on a beam, back arched, arms flung back and chest thrust forward in an unnatural stiff pose, like one of those silver statues on the front of a posh car. It didn't look like Dot at all. Dot was shy and quiet and had given up gymnastics a year ago, because of all the people who insisted on looking at you while you were doing it.

'Gosh, doesn't she look grown-up?' said Mum, and stuck the photo to the fridge. 'You should invite her to visit, Pea-pod. Maybe Clem could bring her, next time he comes up?'

But Pea was afraid to ask. Dot was obviously very busy, after all, what with playing DS with Esme, and being called Dotty now. Pea had an awful feeling that if she did invite her, 'Dotty' might say no.

London life went on.

Tinkerbell 'helped' to redecorate Clover's bedroom walls, with sticky silver fingerprints that had to be turned into an artistic willow tree.

Clover discovered a shop by the park that gave out leaflets on the perils of sulphates – or sulphides, or it could've been phosphates (she forgot) in everyday household products, and said you could stock a bathroom cabinet with things from the kitchen. 'It's very economical, it said in the leaflet. I'm being perfectly Well-Behaved!' she told Mum firmly, replacing all the usual bottles and tubes with jars of honey and foul-smelling tea bags, while wearing a facemask of blueberry yoghurt.

Mum went on asking, 'I did do the right thing,

buying this house, didn't I?' in a plaintive voice, while fishing the toothpaste out of the bin.

Pea, meanwhile, spent hours sitting alone in her attic, staring at the same page of her book. Tinkerbell was merrily causing mayhem, Clover was in yoghurty heaven, Mum was stressed – but Pea was lonely. And she couldn't tell any of them how she felt.

'No stamps? So you are not sending any more postcards to this Dot person, yeah?' Vitória said one afternoon as they were writing the weekly shopping list. Whenever it was Pea's turn to do jobs – stacking the dishwasher, or scrubbing carrots – Vitória would treat her to a tiny cup of coffee afterwards (decaffeinated, or there were headaches). They would sit at the kitchen table, and chatter away about this and that. Vitória was very easy to talk to, Pea had discovered. Pea didn't have to make sure *she* was settling into London, or pretend that she couldn't see a giant red pimple on the end of *her* nose. Vitória didn't pale alarmingly whenever another bill for kitchen chairs or electricity arrived. Vitória didn't need looking after at all.

So it was easy to tell her about Dot, and feeling a tiny bit sad.

Vitória looked thoughtful, then beckoned Pea through the door of her flatlet off the kitchen. Mum had been very stern about them all giving Vitória her privacy, so it felt very grown-up to be allowed properly inside. There was a big bed, covered in purple satiny stuff and mountains of cushions, and another door to a sparkling white bathroom. Vitória fetched her photo album, and they perched on the end of the bed together. There were lots of pictures of Vitória's mum looking very glossy and glam (she was apparently on TV in Brazil, because her new husband owned a TV station; that explained the silver car), and Vitória's sister (who was glossy too), and lots of friends, hugging and laughing.

'I haven't seen some of them in ages,' said Vitória, sighing as she turned the pages. 'But it's not a problem though, innit? 'Cos I made new London friends. Just like you will, yeah?'

Pea wasn't so sure. She'd liked Dot. It didn't seem fair to have to start all over again.

But back in the kitchen she looked at the photo of Dotty on the fridge, and knew Vitória was right. She'd changed too: she was a London Pea now. And a London Pea needed a London best friend.

I WOULD LIKE MY NEW BEST FRIEND TO BE
Friendly
Unusual
Funny
Imaginative (likes books)
Very punctual and not off school being ill a lot
    so I don't have anyone to sit with
Nice to me

Now all she needed to do was find someone who would fit the bill.

CHAPTER 4

THE MESSAGE IN A BOTTLE

The ideal best-friend candidate presented itself the very next day.

Pea was in the back garden, reading an old book from the library called *Lottie and Lisa* that Mum had guessed (correctly) she'd like, when a tatty red-and-blue football suddenly bounced into view, almost knocking the book out of her hands.

It had come from next-door's garden, over the high brick wall.

Pea put down her book, and tentatively threw the ball back over. (It took her two tries: throwing

61

was more of a Tinkerbell sort of thing, and it was a very high wall.)

'Thanks!' shouted a voice.

'You're welcome,' said Pea, feeling very awkward about shouting at someone she couldn't see.

So she ran into the house, up the stairs, and into Clover's room.

'Oi!' shouted Clover, who was sitting in her dressing gown with her feet in a bowl of minty-smelling porridge. 'Careful, I'm detoxifying!'

Pea stepped gingerly around the porridge, and peered out of the window.

The other side of their half-a-house had a garden like the twin of their own, except with neat grass, a climbing frame with monkey bars, and a vegetable patch instead of lumpy paving and a shed. You could see over the wall between the two quite clearly from Clover's orange-and-silver bedroom. And in the garden, beside the faded red-and-blue football, was a person sitting on the grass reading a book. It looked about Pea's age, the person. It had floppy brown hair, and she couldn't tell if it was a boy or a girl.

Pea waved her arm, and knocked on the window.

The person looked up, scanning the sky with a frown. Then the person – it really was impossible to tell if it was a girl or a boy – saw her, smiled widely, and waved too: a proper, excited, pleased-to-meet-you sort of wave.

That was definitely FRIENDLY.

Pea spun about, knocked the porridge bowl so that it splattered up Clover's ankles, hissed, 'Sorry!' to her, and hurried back down to the garden.

But it was starting to rain, and though she called 'Hello?' there was no answer. By the time she'd raced back upstairs to Clover's room (where she was not at all welcome), the next-door garden was empty, and fat raindrops were splashing against the windowpane.

All the same, Pea was thrilled. There was a potential new Dot next door, *and* it had been reading. Pea mentally ticked off 'Imaginative (likes books)' on her 'Best Friend Requirements' list at once.

The next day there was a large sign on Clover's bedroom door, with

Clover's Private Bedroom
Knocking Required

in scrolly writing on it. Pea was only allowed in to hover hopefully at Clover's window as long as she agreed to let Clover paint a stinky yellow mixture onto her head.

'Apparently, the very best thing for hair is a sort of apricot that only grows in India,' Clover said, wiping off a dribble that was running down Pea's neck. 'But the astringent qualities of vinegar and conditioning properties of egg yolks are a good substitute. It said so in my leaflet.'

'Mmm,' said Pea, holding her nose, and noting that Clover hadn't put any eggs or vinegar on her *own* hair.

By the time the person arrived in the garden, Pea's head had dried hard and shiny, like a shell.

Pea waved frantically – but the floppy-haired person didn't even look up. She or he half-heartedly kicked the tatty red-and-blue football around, looking bored.

'You can't go outside like that!' said Clover, rapping on Pea's shiny eggy head as she tried to run out to the garden to shout over the wall.

It took for ever to wash all the egg out, and by the time Pea's hair was clean(ish), the floppy-haired person had gone.

The next day, when Pea sneaked into Clover's room to wait, and then to frantically wave (Clover was in the bath, doing something with orange peel), the person gave her a severe and ominous glare, then went straight back indoors.

It was very confusing.

'It might be a prisoner being held against their will,' said Tinkerbell darkly. 'They could be being hideously tortured for most of the day, and only be allowed out every now and then, for good behaviour. And if anyone sees them waving, back indoors they go for more thumbscrews.'

Pea took this very seriously. She hadn't really believed that Dot had been a secret spy in need of rescue, but this was different: there was definitely something odd going on next door. There was a sign on the red-brick pillar at the end of the drive: a square brass plate, with DR KARA SKIDELSKY & DR G. M. F. PAGET: CHILD PSYCHOLOGY & FAMILY THERAPY etched into the metal. Different people scrunched up the gravelly drive every day – always children, usually with an adult or two to drop them off or pick them up. They always looked worried. Sometimes they were crying. Pea suspected that Dr Kara Skidelsky or Dr G. M. F. Paget was quite capable of keeping one of them behind, for imprisoning purposes.

She began to imagine chains and padlocks, just on the other side of the wall, and resolved to learn semaphore *and* Morse code in case the waving was really a desperate signal for help. Tinkerbell made flags, and they stood at opposite ends of the landing, trying to spell each other's names. Tinkerbell definitely seemed happier, now there was plotting to do to take her mind off Tenby – and Pea remembered that her little sister could be quite kind sometimes, even if her eyes did light up alarmingly whenever she said 'thumbscrews'. But it turned out that semaphore was quite complicated and boring to learn, and there was a very good reason someone had invented text messages instead. Unfortunately, imprisoned persons didn't tend to have mobile phones – and neither did Pea or Tinkerbell.

That afternoon Clover put up a new sign:

Clover's Private Bedroom
No Entry at All to People under 14,
Not Even if You Knock.
GO AWAY!

Banished, they holed up in Tinkerbell's bedroom – Tinkerbell standing on her bed, ear pressed up against the mysterious nailed-up door; Pea kneeling to peer under the bed at that telltale crack of light. There was a piano being played somewhere in the neighbouring house, and the music – the *Moonlight Sonata*, very slow, with the same part being played over and over, always going wrong at the same place – drifted eerily through the wall. They couldn't hear any rattling chains or screams of terror, but the stop-start piano was quite creepy enough.

'We could try un-nailing this door,' said Tinkerbell, poking under a nail with her finger-tip. 'That must go straight into the house next door.'

'Tink, you mustn't, ever!' said Pea, appalled. 'That would be like breaking into their house!'

That wasn't the whole reason. Pea had read *Coraline* last year, and though she knew it was only a story, it seemed best for everyone if the door between the houses stayed nailed shut. Just in case.

There had to be another way of getting a message to the person next door.

When the tatty red-and-blue football bounced into their garden again a few days later, Pea had a brainwave.

ARE YOU A PRISONER?
IF YOU NEED RESCUING, PUT REPLY INSIDE
FOOTBALL AND THROW IT OVER OUR WALL.
love from Pea (the girl next door)

She tucked the note through a small hole in the stitching of the football, and got Tinkerbell to kick it high up in the air, back over the wall.

Then Pea and Tinkerbell knocked on Clover's door, again and again, until it was obvious that *not* letting them in would be much more annoying.

'We have to check something – it's very important,' said Tinkerbell, marching past Clover.

The person was in the garden, idly kicking the red-and-blue football against their wall – so it had definitely found its way into the right garden. But after a while – without a glance up at the window – she or he went inside.

'Maybe they'll notice there's a note inside later?' said Tinkerbell, not sounding convinced.

'What if the horrible imprisoning doctors find it first?' said Pea.

'What?' said Clover, who was reclining on her bed with cucumber slices over her eyes.

Tinkerbell explained their fears for the poor chained-up, thumbscrewed person.

'Are you two mental?' said Clover. 'The person next door isn't horribly imprisoned. They've got a piano. There are monkey bars in their garden. And look – now they're eating an ice cream.'

Pea watched miserably as the person returned to the garden licking a vanilla cone.

It was comforting to think no one was being chained to a wall and thumbscrewed, but now there was no reason at all for the friendly waving to have stopped. Unless, with all those other children coming and going, they simply didn't have time for more friends.

The floppy-haired person probably had a million Dots of his or her own already; no need for a Pea.

Pea sat dejectedly on Clover's bed.

'Did you really want to be friends with this next-door person?' asked Clover, quite gently and ever so slightly Mumlike.

Pea nodded.

'We tried learning semaphore and everything,' said Tinkerbell.

'Then you can't just give up,' said Clover. 'They've got that piano next door. I could go round to ask if I can practise on it – say once a week –

71

and you could come too, and accidentally bump into her. Or him. Whichever it is.'

Pea felt much better now that someone else was in charge of finding her a best friend for a bit.

Clover waited until quarter past two on a Monday afternoon ('because anyone who's at home at quarter past two on a Monday will probably like being distracted by the doorbell – Mum always does'), and scrunched down the gravelly path.

Pea and Tinkerbell waited at the end of the drive, by the red-brick pillar with the engraved brass plate for DR KARA SKIDELSKY & DR G. M. F. PAGET: CHILD PSYCHOLOGY & FAMILY THERAPY. Even without any imprisoning going on beyond it, Pea still found it quite intimidating, for a brass square was almost certainly more important than a blue plaque.

When the front door swung open, they dipped behind the pillar.

Pea could hear Clover's voice, unusually meek,

then another, rather brisk, in reply, and couldn't resist peering out. The person on the doorstep was a pale, elongated lady: long skirt, long cardigan, long strings of beads. Clover looked oddly pink and three-dimensional beside her. They talked quietly for a short time. It all looked very businesslike. They even shook hands.

Then the front door closed, and Clover hurried down the path.

'That was Dr G. M. F. Paget, and the G stands for Genevieve,' Clover told them, once they were safely back inside their own front door. 'She wasn't *very* scary. But she said she was with a patient, and actually quarter past two isn't at all a good time to ring people's doorbells. We should tell Mum she's doing afternoons all wrong. *Anyway*, she said I can play their piano whenever I like! *And* she finishes early on Tuesdays and we can come for afternoon tea tomorrow. All of us. She said she's been meaning to invite us over ever since we moved in. *And*' – Clover beamed at Pea – 'she asked me to give this to "the red-headed girl from the window".'

Clover pressed a folded scrap of paper into Pea's hand.

DEAR PEA (it said),
THANK YOU FOR THE NOTE (I THINK IT WAS FOR ME). I AM NOT A PRISONER BUT I AM QUITE BORED. COME AND VISIT. WE HAVE MONKEY BARS.
FROM SAM

Pea glowed. Her person had a name (a frustrating one, true; if only they were called something helpful like Jack or Julietta), and the waving had been friendly all along, and they hadn't thought she was silly for writing 'love from Pea' on her note or thinking they might be horribly imprisoned.

And tomorrow she would meet them properly, for afternoon tea.

I WOULD LIKE MY NEW BEST FRIEND TO BE

Friendly ✓

Unusual

Funny

Imaginative (likes books) ✓

Very punctual and not off school being ill a lot
    so I don't have anyone to sit with

Nice to me

LIVING NEXT DOOR?

CHAPTER 5

AFTERNOON TEA

Mum emerged from behind the DO NOT DISTURB OR I WILL PROD YOU WITH MY TRIDENT sign on the study door quite late. She was definitely more Mumlike than Marina Coveish about their neighbour-befriending plans.

'Are you sure she invited you, and you didn't just invite yourselves? Is she expecting me to come too? I ought to be writing, really. And what about poor Vitória? What time are you meant to be there?'

They explained – sort of – about Pea's person, and the waving, and the message in the football.

Mum softened. 'So is this Sam a boy or a girl?'

'We don't really know,' said Pea.

'Ooh! A mystery. I like mysteries. Stuff mermaids, then. I'm allowed to take the afternoon off if there's a mystery.'

'Of course you can. It's afternoon tea,' breathed Clover, eyes bright. 'We've never invited anyone round for afternoon tea. It's so very *London*.'

'We should take something,' said Mum, looking dismally at the nutritious things in the kitchen cupboard. 'And it ought to at least look home-made.'

'How about jelly?' said Tinkerbell. 'That's home-made.'

'I suppose, if you absolutely must,' said Mum.

'Though afternoon tea is very sophisticated,' said Clover, 'so don't be all grumpy if it doesn't get eaten.'

Tinkerbell promised sincerely not to mind.

She bought the jelly – strawberry – with her own pocket money, chopped it into cubes, and didn't moan when Vitória said that *she* should be the one to do the bit with the kettle and the boiling water. Tinkerbell spent the evening dipping her nose into the fridge at intervals, to 'monitor setness levels'.

The next morning Clover got up especially early (which meant at the same time as everyone else, really) and put herself in charge of co-ordinating wardrobes.

Pea borrowed Mum's computer to check what time afternoon teas were meant to happen. It said from three o'clock until five, so they each only had a banana for brunch to make sure there was room for scones and tiny sandwiches, like in the photos on the internet. It was hard not to feel hungry after looking at macaroons. Pea distracted herself by mentally listing potential topics of conversation, so that she could plan being spontaneously witty.

Please fill out this short questionnaire so I may assess your suitability for friendship.

1. What is *Sam* short for?
2. Complete the following sentence:
   'Unusual people are . . .'
3. Tell me a joke.
4. What is a prime number?
5. Please share your medical history, including any allergies, occasions of being bedridden, plague, etc.
6. Have you ever done bullying – for example, of people with red hair? (Be honest.)
7. Describe your ideal friend in 3 words: e.g. imaginative, enthusiastic, local.

Then they both sat Tinkerbell down in her bedroom, and made stern noises.

'No shoes on the furniture,' said Clover. 'Or paint. Or slime.'

'If there are sandwiches, you can't take them apart and only eat the nice bits,' said Pea.

'Even if there are green things,' added Clover. 'And don't tell any jokes.'

'Or funny stories about surprising places Wuffly's done a poo.'

'Or stories about poo at all.'

'I don't know where you get these ideas,' Tinkerbell said sweetly. 'As if I'd sabotage us making friends with the neighbours.'

'*Please*, Tink,' said Clover. 'It's important. For Pea. Promise?'

'I promise!'

'*Nose*-promise?' said Pea.

A nose-promise was made by pressing your forefinger to the end of your nose. Nose-promises were only for the solemnest things, and were quite unbreakable.

Tinkerbell pouted, then sighed heavily and squished her nose with her fingertip. 'Nose-promise,' she said.

There was a howl from the kitchen.

They all thudded downstairs, to be met by Vitória, fuming in her fluffy yellow dressing gown.

'So you was just being helpful making this, yeah? This is your story?'

Tinkerbell did her innocent face. Everyone knew what that meant.

It wasn't peanut butter in the bra this time. On the kitchen table was a large glass bowl, filled with wobbly red jelly – and something black, embedded in the centre.

'What you got to say for yourself, huh?'

'Maybe it sort of . . . fell in? Somehow?' Tinkerbell shrugged.

The black thing lit up inside the jelly, and began to play a muffled tune.

'Is that your *phone*?' said Pea.

'I know! In a jelly! I mean, it is creative and everything, but yuck, yeah?'

The surface of the jelly quivered in time with the off-kilter music.

Pea stared at Tinkerbell meaningfully.

'All right, all right,' said Tinkerbell. 'It didn't just fall into the fridge. I did it. I'm that kind of child. You'll probably want to find another family to live with now, Vitória.'

'Yeah, yeah,' said Vitória, 'whatever. My last family a boy called Tomas cut off all his sister's hair and tried to blame it on me. You have to try harder than this if you want to get rid of me, little girl!'

Vitória plunged a hand into the jelly, pulled out her phone, and whirled off to her room, muttering to herself in Portuguese.

'Cut off his sister's hair,' murmured Tinkerbell contemplatively, eyeing Clover.

'Stop that!' said Clover. 'Tink, you can't do that sort of thing. We like Vitória!'

'I like Vitória too. It wasn't personal,' Tinkerbell protested. 'I wrapped the phone up in clingfilmy stuff first: it'll be fine.'

'She doesn't know that! Go and apologize. And sound like you mean it!'

Pea stared at the ruined jelly. It was plainly unrescuable: not even squirty cream and jelly tots would cover up the hand-shaped gouge in the middle. She could picture Dr G. M. F. Paget closing the door in their faces at the mere sight.

Clover spotted her clutching her thumbs, and rubbed her arm soothingly. 'Don't panic, it's better this way – I mean, honestly, who even likes jelly?'

She found a strawberry cheesecake in the freezer, which she promised would look entirely home-made once they'd put it on a plate and poked it a bit.

Pea felt very cheered up.

Then they all got dressed in the outfits Clover had laid out for them. Pea wore Clover's second-best blue felt skirt, with a flowy white top over it to hide where the safety pin was in the waist. Tinkerbell was in jeans, but clean ones without holes in the knees. Clover herself wore the emerald skirt of her Cinderella costume from the Tenby

Royal Christmas production, minus the flouncy nets underneath, and a velvet jacket that used to be Mum's. All three were strung about with charms and beads and trinkets, and Vitória (after much apologizing from Tinkerbell) had been persuaded to do their hair – Clover's in artful coils, Pea's in two fat buns on the top of her head like mouse ears. Tinkerbell's cornrows were adorned with tiny blue flowers on a headband, with a matching bow around Wuffly's collar. Tinkerbell herself looked rather unconvinced, but Wuffly trod on the bow and chewed it to a rag, which perked her up no end.

Mum came out of her study in her usual workday clothes (comfy bottoms and a flannel shirt, with her hair up in pencils), and was sent away to try harder, which took ages. Then there was a last-minute panic over whether Wuffly should have a very swift bath because she seemed to have got jelly in her tail, and who was going to do the bathing, if so, because that wasn't anyone's favourite job, and whether she was invited at all. In the end, Wuffly was left shut in Tinkerbell's room – so she wouldn't bother Vitória – and the Llewellyns lived up to their reputation of being a family who were always a bit late for things.

Pea's heart was in her mouth as they scrunched up the gravelly path. This was it. She was going for tea with her future best friend. She poked nervously at her hairclips, willing the two buns on her head to stay in place.

'Best behaviour, chickens,' whispered Mum as she rang the polished brass doorbell. 'Imagine we're visiting the Queen, and then be even more on your best behaviour than that.'

'Good to meet you at last,' said Dr G. M. F. Paget, shaking Mum's hand on the doorstep, and taking the cheesecake (now artfully manhandled, and with tinned mandarin slices arranged on the top for handmade authenticity). 'I'm Genevieve. Don't you all look nice! Are you going somewhere special later?'

'Um. Yes,' said Clover, shrinking a little in her velvet jacket.

Dr Paget waved an arm towards the front room, and disappeared down the hall, towards what Pea guessed was the kitchen. The whole house was a perfect mirror image of theirs: the same, only with the stairs on the wrong side, and the doors all swapped about. Pea felt as if she had passed through a portal into a parallel world, and would not have been at all surprised if a talking lion had appeared at the top of the stairs to deliver the tiny cucumber sandwiches.

Mum's mobile rang, loudly, in her handbag.

'Gosh, I'm so sorry, I really must— Sorry,' she stuttered. From the look on her face, it was almost certainly the Dreaditor.

Mum answered, sinking onto the bottom step, and Pea followed Clover and Tinkerbell into what was the sun room on their side of the house. This one had heavy dark green wallpaper, and two long sofas of pale golden plush. In the middle of a low coffee table were some mugs, and a small – very small – plate of biscuits. Not even chocolaty ones. There was no sign of scones, or tiny cucumber sandwiches. Or, most importantly, of Sam. Instead, lurking half behind the door, there was another woman, in skinny jeans, a Superman T-shirt and a frown.

'Come in, sit, yes,' she said briskly over her shoulder, poring over a mountain of papers on a narrow desk. 'Dr Skidelsky. Pleased to meet you.'

They sat in an awkward line along one sofa. Pea didn't think she'd met a doctor in a Superman T-shirt before. She had purplish hair too, and chunky oblong glasses, and Pea decided she might not be that scary, even if she was on a brass plaque.

'Our mum's just out there,' said Clover. 'In the hall. On the phone.'

'Mmm?' said Dr Skidelsky. 'Well, if she's happy with that, we can start getting to know one another. Please relax, and help yourself to a biscuit. And don't mind me taking notes – nothing to worry about.'

She sat on the golden sofa opposite, rested a clipboard on her knee, and looked expectantly at the three of them.

Pea thought it was a little bit odd, but she'd never been to afternoon tea before. Mum did often say you couldn't believe everything you'd read on the internet.

Clover introduced them all. Tinkerbell reached forward for a biscuit. Pea gave her a nudge with her elbow, to make sure she only took one. Tinkerbell nudged her back, hard, and one of Pea's hairclips pinged open and landed on the coffee table in the middle of the plate of biscuits.

They all looked at it: yellow and sparkly, sitting on top of a digestive.

Pea's fingers itched to pick it up, but she didn't dare move her head.

'Oops,' said Clover eventually, with a false-sounding laugh, and dipped forward to pick it up, blowing off a few crumbs before clipping it uncomfortably back into Pea's hair, at a random spot near the front.

Dr Skidelsky raised an eyebrow thoughtfully, and began scribbling furiously on her notepad. 'You have very unusual names, girls,' she said, still writing.

'Do you think so?' said Clover.

'We've never noticed before,' said Pea.

'You're totally the first person to ever mention it,' said Tinkerbell.

Dr Skidelsky looked up, nodded to herself, then scribbled some more.

Clover related the familiar old story about how Clovers were lucky, and Tinkerbells might have been Stegosauruses.

'And Pea – is that short for something?'

Pea paused. She had a feeling that Dr Kara Skidelsky, Child Psychologist & Family Therapist, could tell if you were lying – but she so wanted Sam to like her, and there had already been a hairclip

89

in the biscuit plate. She wasn't sure admitting to 'Pwudenthe' would help.

'It's short for Pelagia,' said Tinkerbell, without missing a beat. 'It's Greek for dolphin, or sea-creature. So she's sort of named after a mermaid, really.'

Pea felt her cheeks flush pink.

'Mum did meet Pea's father on a Greek island,' said Clover, her eyes wide, as if she might actually believe her sister was a Pelagia and not a Prudence at all.

'That's where he got lost,' said Tinkerbell. 'Well, not lost. He just sort of left one day, on a boat. We think he might have been a pirate all along.'

Dr Skidelsky nodded, hesitating in her scribbling. 'So you all have different fathers?' she asked. She said it quite benevolently, as if it were more important for them to tell her than it was for her to know.

Pea looked anxiously at the open door, in case next-door neighbours were people Clover wasn't supposed to tell *everything* to, like school secretaries and old men at bus stops. But she could faintly hear Mum still talking on the phone – something about delivering boxes of books to the house for her to sign – and Clover was already launching into another well-worn story.

'Mum met my dad, Dave Duff, when they were at school, and they got married, and then he died in a car accident when I was only a tiny baby.' Clover paused for the usual *oh*s and *how sad*s, but Dr Skidelsky wasn't a usual sort of listener. 'Mum decided that being a tragic widowed single mother aged eighteen sounded awful, so she used the insurance money to buy a round-the-world ticket, and set off with me on an adventure to see where we ended up. A few years later, she met an American called Ewan McGregor – no, not that one – in Greece, and they had a whirlwind romance, but he left the night Pea was born.'

Pea made the appropriate mournful face. (Neither of them were being callous; it was simply that the story of their fathers had been told so many times that it had become like a fairy tale, and not about them at all. Pea knew from books that she was meant to be deeply wounded by his absence, but if she was honest she never really thought about him.)

'I don't expect he was a pirate, really,' said Clover. 'But if we pretend he was, it makes him running away not so depressing for Pea.'

Pea flushed pinker. She'd never exactly thought of it that way.

She scratched her head, where the hairclip Clover had put back in was digging in, and felt an alarming wilting sensation from one of her buns. Tinkerbell's eyes widened urgently. Pea grabbed the bun and held it in place, propping her elbow on her knee as if she was just resting her head. Tinkerbell nodded her approval.

Dr Skidelsky adjusted her glasses, and wrote what seemed to be a very long paragraph.

'And a few years later, of course,' said Clover,

'Mum met Clem. Tink's dad. And he didn't die or sail off in a boat or anything.'

'So – he lives with you?'

Clover shook her head. 'They aren't together any more – haven't been for years. But it's all very friendly. He lets all of us win at Monopoly, not just Tink.'

Tinkerbell nodded in confirmation.

Dr Skidelsky sat back, tucking one hand under her chin. 'It sounds a very exotic upbringing,' she said eventually.

'We have lived in lots of different places,' said Pea, still with her elbow propped awkwardly on one knee, hair-bun clutched in her fist. 'Goa, and Madagascar, and Skegness – all over the world, really, so long as it was by the sea, and Mum could find a job, and people to look after us, and somewhere to stay. We had a Mongolian yurt in Prestatyn. That was *definitely* exotic.'

'Don't forget the commune in Germany,' said Clover darkly, for she tended to remember those days with less rosy spectacles. 'Two hundred and fifty people all sleeping in the same room, compulsory yoga at four a.m., and cheese for breakfast.'

'And ham.' Normally this was a hated memory, but there had only been a banana for brunch, and for a moment the notion of cheese, or ham, or both, left Pea quite distracted. 'We got thrown out for giggling in the middle of Downward Dog. Mum found a boyfriend with a houseboat on the Norwegian fjords after that. That was my favourite.'

Dr Skidelsky blinked several times. 'And which was your favourite?' she asked, turning to Tinkerbell.

'Oh, they were all BT,' said Clover.

'*Before Tink*,' Pea whispered, shooting Tinkerbell an anxious look – for no one liked to be reminded that for a time their family had gone along quite contentedly without them in it. But Tinkerbell was sitting with her ankles crossed, relaxed and smiling beneath her blue-flowered headband, as if somehow everything was going the way she wanted it to without her needing to do very much at all.

'Mum says that's why she's a writer: all that inspirational material to work from,' said Clover proudly, and when Dr Skidelsky looked suitably impressed, she explained all about Mum's books.

'The Mermaid Girls are based on us, actually,' said Clover, tossing her hair and smoothing her hands across her emerald-green skirt.

'Sort of,' said Pea rapidly. 'Ish.'

It said inside the back cover of each book that the Mermaid Girls – blonde blue-eyed Lorelei, pale red-headed Coraly, and dark-haired, dark-skinned Shelley – were based on Marina Cove's own beloved daughters. But Coraly had turned out to be evil, and by book three in the series she was dead, which for Pea had prompted many sleepless nights and long conversations over cocoa about the important line between fiction and reality. (Mum had brought Coraly back as a ghost in the fourth book, which made it easier to bear.)

Dr Skidelsky's pen stopped halfway through a sentence, and she sat back on the sofa. 'You know, I'm not sure one hour a week will be quite enough. There does seem to be rather a lot to work through,' she said, twirling her pen thoughtfully.

'I am *so* sorry,' said Mum, hurrying into the room with her phone still in one hand, holding her other out to shake Dr Skidelsky's. 'Bree Llewellyn. What have my horrible offspring been saying about me?'

Dr Skidelsky smiled thinly, cleared her throat, and began to talk about scheduling regular therapy sessions for each of them individually.

'*Therapy* sessions?' said Mum. 'Um . . . what . . . ?'

Then Dr Paget reappeared, carrying a tray with a teapot and a jug of milk, and – with an unexpected snort of laughter that rattled her long strings of beads – explained to Dr Skidelsky that they were the neighbours, and not people looking for Child Psychology and Family Therapy at all.

'You remember, Kara: Clover knocked on the door to ask about playing the piano yesterday,' she said.

'Did she?' said Mum, looking mortified.

Dr Skidelsky starting writing that down too, until Dr Paget whipped the pen and clipboard out of her hand, and gave her startled face a quick kiss.

'Sorry, ladies,' said Dr Paget, pouring tea. 'We do sometimes get our diaries a little mixed up. Kara teaches at Edinburgh University most weekdays in term-time, so she's away a lot.'

'Let me know if you change your mind, though,' said Dr Skidelsky, still watching Mum keenly from behind her oblong glasses. 'I could write the most fascinating chapter in my next book about your girls . . .'

Mum's teacup rattled in its saucer, and Dr Paget cleared her throat.

Dr Skidelsky stopped talking at once.

They sat in awkward silence.

'Is Sam here?' asked Pea.

'Oh, so you've met our Sams?' said Dr Skidelsky with a smile.

'There's been some very inventive communication going on, I gather,' said Dr Paget. 'Go on, Pea, my love – you don't have to sit around here with the boring grown-ups.'

Pea stood up awkwardly, still clutching the unfurling lump of hair, and once out in the hallway managed to stuff it back into the hairclip. She hesitated, not sure if she was meant to look upstairs, before a movement caught her attention.

Sam was in the kitchen.

Pea hurried down the corridor, rippling her fingers through the air to fix how it felt to be her, there and then, on the brink of best-friendship, so she could remember it always.

'Hi!' she said, waving in her most friendly way.

Sam didn't look up. She – or he – was wearing jeans and a yellow T-shirt with a robot on it, which wasn't helpfully boyish or girlish. His – or her –

floppy head was entirely focused on the strawberry cheesecake, dotted with tinned mandarin slices, which she – or he – was forking their way through with great determination.

'Sam, can you bring in that cheesecake?' shouted Dr Paget's voice from the front room.

Sam looked up, noted Pea's presence, and began eating even more quickly.

'It's me!' said Pea.

'Well, duh,' said Sam, between mouthfuls.

'From next door? Pea? I sent the message over the wall?'

Sam glared. 'You mean, you were the one who ripped a hole in my football?'

Pea bit her lip. This was not at all how this conversation was meant to go. Sam was meant to be Friendly, and Imaginative, and Nice To Her. They were going to go on the monkey bars.

'There was already a hole in it,' she said, her voice going faint. 'I didn't rip it. At least, I didn't mean to. I'm very sorry if I did.'

'Sam! Cheesecake! Now!' came another shout from the corridor.

Sam looked Pea up and down, then stared directly at her hair. As if impelled by the gaze, the hairclip began to slip and slide, and slowly the whole bun unravelled itself, leaving half her hair knotted up, and the other half lying across her face like a curly curtain.

Sam smirked. Then she – or he – licked the fork, dropped it back into the drawer with all the clean ones, and picked up the half-eaten cheesecake.

'Shoo! Argh! Nooo!' Sam shouted in a startlingly loud voice, and raced past Pea along the corridor. 'A dog! A dog just got into the kitchen, and chewed it right off the plate! Look!'

Chaos ensued.

Dr Paget hurried into the kitchen to de-dog it for Dr Skidelsky (who was not a dog person).

Clover shouted at Tinkerbell for not locking Wuffly up properly.

Mum's phone rang again, and she told the Dreaditor to shush up and leave her alone – then called her straight back to apologize in her best 'nice author' voice.

Pea protested that she really, truly, hadn't seen a dog.

Sam gave her a malevolent stare, and said that with all that hair over her face she probably couldn't see anything.

'Sam!' gasped Dr Skidelsky. 'How dare you be so rude to a guest?'

Then she peered suspiciously over the top of her glasses, and located a telltale splodge of strawberry sauce and a mandarin-coloured smear on Sam's cheek.

Sam was sent upstairs in disgrace, Tinkerbell demanded an apology for Wuffly, Mum had to tell the Dreaditor to call her back because of all the shouting, Clover asked when she could next come over to play the piano, Mum shouted at her too, and Pea burst into tears.

Dr Paget offered them more tea, but didn't look all that disappointed when Mum said no.

They fled down the drive, up the crazy paving, and back through their own raspberry-red front door, where Mum pulled everything out of the fridge and threw it on the kitchen table, as they were all far too hungry to wait for something to cook.

Everyone dug in, except for Pea. She sat miserably on a kitchen chair, hiding her face behind her hair-curtain, too upset to eat. It was bad enough not having a best friend, but thinking you'd found one who turned out to be mean was much, much worse.

'So how was your next-door visiting?' said Vitória brightly, coming to hear what all the noise was about.

Mum made a small, hopeless, deflated noise.

'I think,' said Tinkerbell, eating ruined jelly and contemplating Pea with a glint in her eye, 'that it couldn't possibly have gone any better.'

CHAPTER
6

MERMAIDS IN KILTS

The summer ended, and it was time to start at their new schools. Tinkerbell would go to the local primary, which was only a walk away. Clover and Pea were enrolled at Greyhope's, which they had to get to by bus.

Pea was moderately terrified.

At first, the prospect of school had been a good distraction from Sam next door, who never even looked up at Clover's window now, except to stick his or her tongue out, or to swing possessively on the monkey bars. But as the days were ticked off the calendar, the new-best-friend issue suddenly became very pressing indeed. Dot had always been there to sit next to in the classroom and on trips (so there was no possibility of her being paired up with Janice McMenemin, who had verrucas, and spat). She couldn't remember *making* friends with Dot. She was always just there, a solid, dependable presence by her side.

'You're lucky, Pea-pod,' said Mum soothingly. 'Everyone will be new at your school, going up to Year Seven. Clover and Tink have to join classes who all already know each other, and they're not worried.'

But it was all right for Clover, who could Mummify friends without even thinking about it. Tinkerbell said she didn't care at all about starting her new school, almost as if she didn't believe it would happen. For Pea, knowing she wouldn't be the only lost new girl didn't help; it just meant more competition. Locating a new Dot when you were just another new girl – one with that chin, and that hair, and that *something* that pristine girls rejected on instinct – was a scary prospect.

The one bright spot was the Greyhope's uniform. It was brown and mustard yellow, and included a yellow kilt, a vehemently striped blazer and an official stripy hair ribbon that had to be ordered in advance from one particular shop. Clover had declared the whole thing 'vomitous', but the moment Pea saw it, she launched into research mode. She read all the *Malory Towers* and *St Clare's* books that were in Kilburn library. They were old and out of date, and about a boarding school, but everyone in them was comfortingly either good or evil. Her imagined Greyhope's filled up with healthy types named Marjorie, who played lacrosse with their tuck boxes. She was confident one of them would take her under their wing.

I WOULD LIKE MY NEW BEST FRIEND TO BE ♡
Friendly
Unusual
Funny

Imaginative (likes books)
Very punctual and not off school being ill a lot
    so I don't have anyone to sit with
Nice to me
~~LIVING NEXT DOOR?~~
Exactly like Sally from Malory Towers

'You look like sliced poo. In custard,' said Tinkerbell, waving them off on their first morning.

The hopefulness began to wear off Pea as she sat on the bus in her knee-high brown socks, surrounded by normal people in trainers eating Egg McMuffins and texting. Suddenly Clover's approach looked like the right one, after all. She had viewed the colour scheme and itchy nylon as a challenge: hitched up the kilt to shorten it, flipped the collar of the blazer and rolled up the sleeves, and wore so many ribbons tied in knotty bows all over her sophisticated first-day hairdo as to be sarcastic.

She did smell a little bit of mushrooms – there had been a last-minute preparatory facepack of them that morning, mixed with milk – but otherwise she looked entirely the part of the charming, slightly rebellious new girl.

'If you get stuck, just tell people you're my sister,' said Clover, cheerfully waving goodbye to the top row of the bus.

But Greyhope's was red-brick and full of girls who didn't carry lacrosse sticks *or* wear their hair ribbons sarcastically. Hardly any of them were wearing hair ribbons at all. They all seemed to know how to find Chemistry 3 and the art block, too.

Pea hovered close behind Clover as they emerged from the secretary's office five minutes after the first lesson had begun, clutching a confusing mess of maps and timetables. At Tenby Primary, all the lessons had been in one place with Mrs Davies. Now, she would have to find her way from room to room, and there was a different teacher for each subject.

'STOP!' came a bellow down the hall. 'You! Blonde girl!'

Clover turned, with her most charming smile.

'This hair is inappropriate,' said Mrs King, acting deputy head, whose own was metallic grey and short, like a mumsy robot. 'The uniform is not to be disrespected. And those nails are *not* regulation.'

'Really?' said Clover. 'Sorry, we're new. I'm Clover, this is Pea – pleased to meet you. I'll do them all the same colour tomorrow if you like, but I thought a rainbow was just perfect for a first day.' She wiggled her Technicolor fingertips (courtesy of Vitória's extensive varnish collection: purple, blue, green and yellow, and scarlet for the thumbs).

Mrs King was evidently immune to rainbows. Pea watched as she marched Clover off to the medical room, for scrubbing.

Then she was completely on her own.

By the time she'd found her first lesson – history, with Ms Leonard – the only available seat was on a table at the front, with three shiny bowed heads already sitting together.

Lilly had the longest plait Pea had ever seen, and clever eyes, like a cat.

Elly had a pencil case in the shape of a swan.

Molly was round and wore glasses with red plastic frames.

Since they were already a three – which meant one was spare; that was always how it worked – they seemed ideal candidates for friendship. At least one of them had to be a little bit Sally-like.

Pea waited politely for the welcoming smiles, and offers to join in practical jokes and midnight feasts. But Lilly, Elly and Molly had apparently read different sorts of school stories, where the students ignored the new girl, and talked loudly about what Charlie said to Mali about Susan Woodiman's shoes all last year, oh my days! And since Pea had never met Susan Woodiman, and shoes were never her strong point at the best of times, it was difficult to know how to contribute.

Even if they were all new to Greyhope's, it turned out all the other girls knew each other from their old schools. Pea felt very lost indeed.

'You've got nice handwriting,' she offered eventually to Molly, who was nearest.

'Thanks!' said Molly.

Lilly's clever eyes narrowed.

Molly tilted her chair away from Pea, just a fraction. And that was that.

For the rest of the morning Pea resolved to only sit at tables where the next-door seat was empty, so that a suitable Dot-replacement could easily find her instead.

But no one came to sit beside her. No one, all morning.

Lunch was held in the huge echoey cafeteria. Pea joined the queue, then found out she was meant to have picked up a tray, and had to go back to the end of it again. Then she had to do the same to get a knife and fork (though there weren't any knives, so she got a spoon instead) and a cup for water. By the time she got to the front, all that was left was the scrapy burned bit from the bottom of a lasagne, and some green beans.

Then she had to find somewhere to sit.

Pea stood still in the noise and bustle, and gazed helplessly around the mass of heads and tables. She spotted Clover at the centre of a table full of older girls, wiggling her naked fingernails in the air as she regaled them with the dramatic tale of scrubbed hands in the medical room. But it was definitely not right for a Year Seven girl to go and sit with them. Pea steeled herself, and sat in the big empty space at the end of Lilly, Elly and Molly's table; near enough to almost be part of the conversation, far enough for it not to seem over-confident.

But Lilly, Elly and Molly went on talking about shoes, and shops, and all the fun things they'd done together in the holidays, as if Pea weren't there at all.

No one would share Pea's 'Dairy Products'

worksheet in French, leaving her stranded with *le lait longue conservation*. No one would pass her the netball, resulting in a 23-0 victory for the other side (though Pea had to admit that passing her the ball probably wouldn't have changed that).

All in all, it was a rather bruising first day.

Clover saw her slumped shoulders at the bus stop, and stayed generously silent on the bus ride home. But the instant she had Mum and Vitória as an audience, she gushed about her *fabulous* first day.

'I've got three friends already, and they're called Tash and Zelda and Elena. Getting told off by the head for having naughty fingernails was the perfect start – thank you, Vitória! After that everyone was awfully curious about the new girl. They all gathered round me in a circle and took pictures for Facebook. It was a bit like being a celebrity, I expect. Anyway, I *love* being a Greyhope's girl. It's so . . . *Londonish*.'

Tinkerbell, meanwhile, had apparently fared even worse than Pea (badly enough to have absconded at lunch time, only to be found by Vitória in the sweet shop and marched back to the head teacher's office) – but she didn't seem to care. She had *My First Atlas* propped on her knees, and appeared to be drawing in a few new continents.

'I'm not bothering to make friends,' she told Pea, on hearing about the empty chair. 'Doesn't seem worth it.' When Pea asked why not, Tinkerbell simply tapped her nose ominously.

'Don't be blue, my starlings,' said Mum, throwing marshmallows at their heads unhelpfully. 'If the children at your new schools are anything like the ones I met today, you'll make friends in no time.'

In between chapters she gave Creative Writing workshops to schools, and they always left her frothy, like milkshake. She had come home with a pile of handwritten stories, and even a fan letter.

Dear Marina Cove,
I have read all your books about
the Mermaid Girls lots of times.
You are my favourite writer ever
in the world. When I grow up
I would like to be you and/or a
mermaid.
Love from Zhou (your biggest fan)

'She was such a sweetie, that girl,' said Mum. 'Wrote me a story about mermaids who turned red because they all ate nothing but tomatoes. Genius! They were all brilliant kids, though – brimful of ideas.'

'Can I change schools and go to that one instead, then?' asked Pea.

But Mum poked a marshmallow into Pea's mouth, and smiled the idea away.

The next day Clover went to school ribbonless, with her fingernails painted a quiet shade of pink.

'Don't stress so much, Pea,' she said, before disappearing into the crowd. 'Just be yourself!'

Pea suspected that being *Clover* would be much more effective. She tried out all Clover's usual Mummification techniques: bright smile, eye contact, a light giggle as she 'dropped' her spoon at lunch time and had to go and fetch another one (though if it was working, someone else would have offered to do it for her). She even tried washing her face in mushrooms – though from the look of the bathroom cabinet, Clover had quietly returned to using ordinary soap and shampoo without eggs in. But Lilly, Elly and Molly were utterly immune.

By the end of the week she was almost tempted to try making friends with horrible Sam next door again.

Mum suggested they all invite new friends from school over on Saturday afternoon, but Pea and Tinkerbell hadn't made any. To Pea's surprise, Clover said Tash and Zelda and Elena couldn't possibly come over either, as she had promised Dr

Paget she would practise on the piano that day.

'This is crazy business,' said Vitória, making Volcano Toasties for lunch to cheer Pea up as Clover's unsteady piano scales floated through the wall between the houses. 'I know you is a nice person, right? But these new girls at this school, they don't know you so well. So you have to show them some things about yourself, so they can see why they want to be friends with you, yeah?'

Pea hadn't thought about it that way round, and pondered long and hard about what she had to offer as a friend.

The next week, in their first English lesson, Pea sat with Lilly, Elly and Molly again. She waited until Mr Ellis handed out their reading diaries, then said, quite casually, 'My mum's a writer.'

After all, if she couldn't go to school with Marina Cove's biggest fan, perhaps the *Mermaid Girls* could still help to single her out.

'Mine writes for *The Times*,' said Lilly.

'Mine works at the BBC,' said Elly.

'Mine's the managing director of a chain of high-street shops,' said Molly, 'which means I get a twenty-five per cent discount card.'

Pea bit her lip. 'But mine's *famous*,' she said. 'Marina Cove? *Mermaid Girls*?'

Pea could see the flicker of recognition: the way Elly and Molly's eyes slid to Lilly's, to see if she would grant permission for them to be impressed.

'It sounds *vaguely* familiar,' Lilly said, looking Pea up and down with a little less frost.

But at the lesson's end, Pea heard whispers: 'Such a liar,' and 'Not even the same last name,' and no one would even look at her all afternoon.

Clover found her weeping at the bus stop, and made soothing noises. But Pea knew her big sister – who had abandoned twirly hairdos and painted fingertips, and regaled Mum and Vitória every night with funny things Tash had said, or the Londonish brilliance of Zelda – couldn't possibly understand.

117

'No no no,' said Vitória, after she had sent Tinkerbell to bed. 'I was meaning, it is about what sort of person *you* are, not who your mum is!'

Pea went up to her attic, and began scouring all her favourite books for help. Once she'd started re-reading the Harry Potters, her mistake seemed obvious.

14 September

Dear Diary,

I think what I have been doing wrong is looking for a friend who is too much like me. Really I am much more a Hermione type of person than a Harry. And I have Weasley hair! So from now on I'm going to look for a heroic, main-characterish sort of person who I can be sidekick to. That way we can have adventures but someone else can do all the hard parts with danger, swords, decision-making, etc.

But it wasn't at all helpful. She kept her eyes peeled for lightning scars, and dropped a few casual references to owls, but that seemed to make people even less keen to be her friend.

By the end of the second week Pea had lost all hope.

She went to Clover's bedroom after school on Friday to peer into next-door's garden, just in case there was an apologetic, entirely transformed Sam waving madly up at her window. But instead there was only Clover, cutting pictures of shoes out of a magazine and lining them up next to her real ones, singing *The Sun'll Come Out Tomorrow* to herself in an unusually soft, quavery voice, surrounded by soggy tissues.

'What's wrong? Shall I fetch Mum? Or Vitória? Do you need a glass of water?'

Clover shook her head, and blinked up at Pea with big red eyes under her sad, too-tidy hair. 'I think I'm broken, Pea,' she croaked between sobs. 'I've gone all unClovered. I don't think I know how to be me in London.'

Now that she was properly looking, Pea saw that it was true: Clover did not seem herself. It was as if someone had gone around her with a pair of scissors and cut off all her edges.

'I am nice, aren't I, Pea?'

There was still a sign on Clover's door that said *GO AWAY!* and Pea's hair had never completely recovered from the eggs and vinegar – but Pea nodded all the same.

'Then why haven't I got any friends?' Clover sniffed.

'But you have!' said Pea, bewildered. 'You've got Tash and Zelda and Elena! They took photos for Facebook! They're Londonish and brilliant!'

Clover hung her head. 'I made it all up. I haven't made any friends at all! The girls in London all wear lacy bras that are pink or yellow or spotty, not ordinary white ones. And they have matchy knickers. And they all like sport, and bands I don't know, and they go to Starbucks together at the weekends, without inviting me – and anyway, we're being too Well-Behaved for coffee shops. *And* they said I smelled like mushrooms.'

Pea clutched Clover's thumbs for her, and felt tears prickling her own eyes. Pea was not at all sure she was entirely Pea in London, either. She hadn't written a new story for days, and had instead spent much of the previous evening trying to fashion a bottom-length plait out of a pair of tights and an old woolly scarf. She hadn't even emailed Clem; it was too difficult to think of things to say that didn't sound miserable.

Tinkerbell appeared in the doorway, took one look at the pair of them, and sat down, closing the door very firmly behind her. 'Well?' she said in a serious voice, folding her arms expectantly.

Pea looked at the weeping Clover and the stern-faced Tinkerbell, and thought about the bucket of sand on the patio, and the printed-off picture stuck to the fridge.

'I think I understand now about the handcuffs, and the jelly, and you getting yourself lost every five minutes,' said Pea slowly.

'And never really wanting to come to London at all,' sniffed Clover, lowering her voice so that no one outside might accidentally hear.

'Finally,' said Tinkerbell. 'So are you on my side now?'

'I don't know,' said Pea. 'I mean, I do like my attic.'

'It's not Mum's fault,' said Clover. 'And Vitória's lovely. And we're not in a yurt in Prestatyn.'

'I liked that yurt!' said Pea.

'You didn't when you were living in it. You just don't remember it properly. It wasn't all fun and adventures, all that moving around. We were always in the way, in other people's houses, taking up space, living out of suitcases and saying goodbye all the time. Even Mum didn't like it. She used to cry and cry after you went to sleep. Trust me, we are *loads* better off now than when you were tiny.'

'But . . . ?' said Tinkerbell.

Clover reached for another tissue. 'Everything's awful. My bedroom's still orange. I haven't got a yellow bra and matchy knickers. No one likes me!'

'And if they don't like *you*, they'll *never* like me,' said Pea.

Clover sniffled. 'What's the point of having a famous writing mum if you don't get to live the fairy-tale ending?'

'*Exactly*,' said Tinkerbell.

'But what can we do?'

Tinkerbell looked very pleased with herself. 'I've got a plan.'

'I don't think a jelly sort of plan is going to help, Tink,' said Pea.

'Forget that,' said Tinkerbell. 'We need to get more ambitious. Remember when we went to afternoon tea next door? How you told Dr Paget about moving house loads of times, BT?'

Pea nodded, then frowned. 'Are you trying to say we were better off BT?'

Clover lifted her head. 'Please don't run away, Tink. That's not what we meant. We quite like you, really.'

Tinkerbell rolled her eyes. 'I'm not the one who has to go, idiot. It's not BT we have to go back to. It's BM.'

'Before Mum?' said Clover, confused.

Pea's eyes grew wide. 'Before Marina,' she breathed.

'Before *Mermaids*,' said Tinkerbell. 'Those whiny fishy books are the only reason we're stuck here in London. So if we want to go back home, all we have to do is get rid of them. Like nits. We need to get de-mermaiding. Un-mermaidify. Ex-merminate!'

Pea gasped. Tinkerbell was right: that was why everything had changed! If there were no more mermaids, they could go back – back home to Tenby, and Dot, and their old life . . .

'But how?' asked Clover.

Tinkerbell gave them a stare. 'Why do I have to think of everything? I'm only seven!'

CHAPTER
7

EX-MERMINATE!

Despite her protests, Tinkerbell's plans for ex-mermination were frighteningly detailed. She had created list after list, heavily illustrated in coloured pencils, and kept the pages hidden in *My First Atlas*, reasoning that it was the sort of big dull book that not even Pea would be likely to look at.

'They're only suggestions, really,' she said as Clover and Pea pored over them on her bedroom floor. Wuffly stood guard at the top of the stairs, in case of a curious Vitória. 'We can all make up new ones.'

Clover held up a gruesome drawing of a severed arm wearing a wristwatch.

'I thought Wuffly might dig it up in the garden,' explained Tinkerbell. 'Then we'd have to move, 'cos who wants to live in a house where there are random bits of dead people under the patio?'

Clover looked sick.

'Where were you going to find a severed arm?' asked Pea warily.

'The internet?' Tinkerbell shrugged. 'Or sometimes they turn up in loaves of bread and cans of Coke. I saw it on TV. Though that's usually fingers, not whole arms. It could be a finger. The picture *is* just for illustration.'

'And this?' said Pea, holding up a drawing of a green-faced monster with huge teeth, headed ZOMBIE INVASION.

'That's you,' said Tinkerbell. 'Dressed up like a zombie. I thought you could run around the house at night making spooky noises, so Vitória would be too scared to live here and there'd be no one to look after us.'

'Why don't *I* get to be the zombie?' said Clover.

126

Her pout was understandable – for had Pea played Cinderella on the Tenby Royal stage? She had not.

'I gave you the speaking role,' said Tinkerbell quickly. 'Lots of screaming and waving your arms about in terror. Thought that was more your thing than Pea's.'

Pea nodded encouragingly. 'You convinced me you'd made lots of friends at school, after all. That was very good acting.'

Clover perked up.

'Won't work anyway,' said Tinkerbell, throwing the page in the bin. 'Vitória's not very scareable. I've been dangling plastic spiders outside her window and putting fake bats in her knicker drawer for months. She doesn't seem fussed.'

'Tink!'

'Don't get all Big Sistery about it. I've stopped now. Anyway, scaring Vitória away isn't going to get rid of the *Mermaid Girls*.' Tinkerbell sniffed, flicking through the scattered papers. 'Most of these are no good, really. That one was *never* going to work.' She tore up a drawing of what appeared to be the three of them weeping over a grave, with FAKE MARINA COVE'S DEATH? written underneath, and stuffed that into the bin too. 'We need new ideas. Pea, I think you should do something clever and writerish. Like, *you* could write the new *Mermaid Girls* book instead of Mum. We could swap hers for your rubbish version at the last minute, and the Dreaditor would yell so much Mum'd never want to see her ever again. What do you think?'

'Why would my *Mermaid Girls* book be rubbish?' said Pea.

'On purpose!' said Tinkerbell hastily. 'Only because you'd made a special effort to write rubbishly. If you wanted to write a good book about fish-women, you totally could. But that wouldn't really help.'

'I suppose I could try,' said Pea, picking at a tuft in the carpet.

'And Clover, maybe you could do some acting at Dr Paget. Like, you could cry a lot instead of playing her piano, and tell her how miserable you are at school. That would make Mum feel super-guilty about making us move.'

'It's a bit harsh, Tink,' said Clover doubtfully.

Tinkerbell folded her arms. 'Look, are you two on the ex-merminating team or not?'

Pea looked at Clover. Clover looked at the smudgy silver flowers on her orange walls. 'We're on the team,' she sighed.

'Nose-promise?'

Clover and Pea exchanged reluctant glances, but Tinkerbell was looking quite fierce, and neither of them wanted to argue. They pressed their fingers to their noses.

'Nose-promise,' they chorused.

'Good,' said Tinkerbell. 'Now go away and think of some more plans, because I've had to do it all by myself so far and it's very tiring.'

And they were sent away, with strict instructions not to say a word about the plan to Mum or Vitória or Clem, or even Dr Paget next door.

Pea went to her attic and attempted to write a shockingly bad story about mermaids, just to see if she could.

Beryl the mermaid was fed up. Living under-water made her fingertips go all wrinkly, like when you stay in the bath too long, and wearing a bra made out of shells was really uncomfy (and not at all supportive for a C-cup either). Also the bit where her tail transformed into legs again because she was on land hurt loads and made her cry out loud, 'Ah me! Why must I be so accursed?'

One time when she was lying on the sand shouting this, a boy came along and heard her. He was very muscular but also skinny, and his eyes were shiny like blue diamonds, if diamonds can be blue. (LOOK THIS UP.) Luckily he was quite far away and she could put her trousers on over her new legs before he got too close.

'What was that you were saying about being accursed?' he said.

130

> 'Oh, nothing, I was just singing a song by Beyoncé,' Beryl lied, gazing into his twinkly eyes, which were like the sea as well as diamonds.

It *was* bad. Pea suspected it was even more bad than she'd meant. Flicking through her notebook at all her half-started stories, she wondered if perhaps quite a lot of them might be bad too. It was because of London, definitely. Tinkerbell was right: everything would be better if they could only move back to Tenby.

The next day was Saturday. Pea wrote Clem a long, extra-cheerful email about how busy they all were on an important project, but how they hoped to see him soon. Clover played the piano next door, and promised she'd been very weepy and glum to Dr Paget. Then Tinkerbell (after much muttering between the sisters, and pooling of their resources) announced that she'd been saving up her pocket money, and *desperately* wanted to spend it on a new book.

It was the sort of statement that Mum could never resist. They walked through the park with Wuffly to Sunflower Books, the tiny little bookshop next door to the fancy bakery. Tinkerbell pinned Mum in a corner, and Clover and Pea set to work in the children's section, removing all copies of the *Mermaid Girls* books they could find, and hiding them in unlikely places where they were sure no one would look, like the 'Fishing' section.

Pea found it thrilling. It was exactly like being a spy with a mission – especially when the tweedy-skirted lady who ran the shop began following them around, mouth puckered with suspicion. Clover had to pretend to be terribly interested in fishing, to distract her while Pea hid a few more copies of *Mermaid Girls 2: Deep Water* in amongst the detective fiction.

'Oh, hello again, I thought you looked familiar!' Mum's voice rang out across the shop.

Pea peered out from behind 'Poetry in Translation', to see Tinkerbell looking thunderous.

Mum was beaming at a tiny Chinese girl with smooth black hair, and a smartly dressed woman Pea guessed was her mother.

'Oh yes, she hasn't stopped talking about it since you visited her school,' said the woman. 'She's such a fan of the *Mermaid Girls* books.'

'*Biggest* fan,' said the girl quietly, but with resolve.

'I think you might have competition there,' said Mum fondly. 'My own daughters are here – somewhere – and they absolutely have to like my books best of anyone; it's in my contract. Ah, Pea! There you are. Come and say hello to – I'm sorry, sweetheart, I can't remember your name.'

Clover gave Pea a shove, and she stumbled forward.

'Zhou,' said the girl. She was the one who had written the fan letter, Pea realized – and the story about the tomato-eating mermaids. Her name was pronounced like a softer-sounding 'Jo': Pea had to keep repeating it over and over under her breath till it sounded right.

'Are you really Marina Cove's daughter?'

Pea nodded, feeling her face go pink under Zhou's enthralled gaze.

'You've got hair just like Coraly,' breathed Zhou, reaching up her hand as if she wanted to touch it.

'Mum did base the character on me,' Pea said, glowing.

She could feel Tinkerbell's furious eyes burning into her from her hiding place behind 'Military History', and knew she would think this was a perfect opportunity for ex-mermination. But Pea was not used to being stared at with such an expression of captivated wonder. It was lovely. It must be what being a real mermaid was like.

'Did you say Marina Cove?' said the tweedy-skirted bookshop lady. 'We've got lots of her books, just over here . . .'

'Um,' said Pea, shooting Tinkerbell an urgent look – because there were lots of Marina Cove's books in the shop; just not in the places you might expect.

Tinkerbell shrugged back, eyes wide with panic.

'Oh, is that the time?' said Clover, emerging from the 'Fishing' section and staring at her wrist, even though she wasn't wearing a watch. 'Busy busy, so much to do, lovely to meet you, byeeee!'

Tinkerbell leaped out and grabbed Mum's arm. Clover threw a Mummifying smile over her shoulder as she pushed Mum's bottom out through the door, insisting that Mum had made her promise to get her back to her writing desk before lunch. Pea gave Zhou an apologetic wave goodbye through the window.

'That's nice, that you made a little friend in the shop,' said Mum to Pea when they got home.

Pea smiled proudly. Then Tinkerbell trod on her foot and gave her a bunchy-mouthed glare. Pea remembered that she wasn't meant to be making friends any more, and mumbled, 'Um, no, not really,' before fleeing to her attic to think about ex-mermination.

It was hard to focus, though. Pea's eyes kept drifting to the page in her notebook with the 'Best Friend Requirements' list, wondering if she should change it to:

Imaginative (likes Mermaid Girls books, especially Coraly)

– although, of course, if Tinkerbell's plotting worked out, there would be no more *Mermaid Girls* books for anyone to like.

No more Coraly, even as a ghost.

No more Marina Cove.

It was a troubling thought. Pea loved Marina Cove nearly as much as she loved Mum. Marina was glamorous and mysterious, and proof that it was possible to write and write and try and try, and if you kept doing those, one day there might be books on a shelf in a shop with, if not exactly your own name, one you'd picked. (The Dreaditor had said Bree Llewellyn was too long for book covers, and sounded like cheese, and people who weren't Welsh couldn't say it properly; that's why she was Marina Cove.) Lately, thanks to Tinkerbell, Pea had settled on her own new pen name: Pelagia Cove. That would look good on a blue plaque. Perhaps they'd have to hang two of them on the brick pillar at the end of the crazy paving.

That is, if Marina Cove kept writing long enough to have a blue plaque . . .

Pea didn't sleep very well that night.

Early the next morning she found Mum eating buttery toast in the study in her dressing gown, in the midst of inventing underwater fire-caves ('because my feet were freezing last night, and I've never really tackled the whole Mermaids vs. Central Heating issue till now').

She had a definite spark in her eye; that unsquashable smile that always appeared whenever a book was going really, really well.

Usually it made Pea beam, but today she felt her stomach go watery with guilt. Underwater fire did sound clever. It would look brilliant on the book cover.

She made Mum a cup of Special Writing Tea (1 sugar, for a morning) in the spotty WE ♥ MUM mug, and thought about how much she would miss that being her job if it ever stopped.

Vitória got up, and filled the house with the delicious smell of brewing coffee. If they left London, Vitória would be sure to go off and make coffee for some other family. Pea would miss her, too.

She put the milk back in the fridge, and saw the printed-off Dotty photograph still pinned there under shopping lists and Tinkerbell's 'Stickers for Good Behaviour' sheet (which was blank). Even if they went back to Tenby, it wouldn't be the same at all. Pea would still have to start again, making a new best friend in another new school.

Pea tiptoed upstairs and hunted out Clover, who was still bundled under her duvet, but not asleep (despite shouting 'I'm asleep' through her bedroom door).

After a long whispery talk they agreed that Tinkerbell's ex-merminating plan, while inventive, was a terrible idea.

'What we really want is for Mum to write *more* books, not fewer,' said Clover. 'How else am I going to get a yellow bra and matchy knickers?'

'But we nose-promised,' said Pea unhappily.

Clover yawned. 'I'm fourteen. I'm too old for nose-promising. One outgrows these things, Pea – you'll see.'

'Is eleven too old for nose-promising?'

'Could be.' Clover looked at Pea assessingly. 'You're quite brainy; that might speed it up. Let's say yes.'

'So we don't have to get rid of Marina Cove and the *Mermaid Girls* after all?'

Clover wrinkled her nose at her orange walls, and Pea half expected her to change her mind again, but Clover seemed strangely resolved.

'Nope. In fact, I think we should do the opposite.'

'But what do we tell Tink?'

'Best not to. She'll probably forget all about it – you know what she's like.'

Pea did, and was not convinced.

Clover spent the rest of Sunday morning 'resting', and the afternoon at Dr Paget's, though not much *Moonlight Sonata* drifted through the walls.

Pea spent the day with Tinkerbell, playing Monopoly to distract her from looking up 'book burning' on the internet.

Mum decided on cakes from the fancy bakery for that night's pudding, because the underwater fire-caves had turned out so brilliantly.

She came home even more overflowing with happiness.

'Guess what, my darlings!' she said, plonking cake boxes down on the kitchen table. 'When I was passing, I got talking to the nice lady who runs the bookshop we went to yesterday. Apparently all day yesterday people were buying my books – not just children either; all sorts of unlikely-looking people who said they'd never seen the books before but now they had, they knew someone who'd like them. She said she'd never sold so many.'

Tinkerbell hid her grumpy face behind a cake box.

'So the bookshop lady's asked me to come in and do a book-signing. Next Saturday! Apparently that nice girl Zhou who you talked to, Pea – it was her idea. How brilliant is that, my sweeties?'

Mum twirled off with Vitória, demanding wardrobe advice.

Pea looked at Clover nervously, then they both looked at Tinkerbell.

Tinkerbell licked chocolate off the top of a glistening éclair, and produced an unexpected and very devious grin.

'Yep. It's going to be *brilliant*.'

CHAPTER 8

ZHOU

On Monday Pea was back at school, feeling as lonely as ever. But the week whizzed by. Preparing for a book-signing turned out to be an all-hands-on-deck affair. There were phone calls to be made, photographs to be taken of Mum looking especially Marina-ish, posters and invitations to be printed off and posted through letter boxes – for, as Mum said, how awful would it be if no one came to ask for a book to be signed?

'*Awfully* awful,' agreed Tinkerbell, her eyes lighting up ominously as she volunteered to be post-person.

Pea followed her to the end of the road, where Tinkerbell ceremoniously deposited all the invitations in someone else's bin. After a suitable wait, they went home again.

An hour later, Pea offered to take Wuffly for a walk, insisting that Clover came too.

'Do I *have* to?' she moaned. 'I'm *busy*.'

She moaned even more when Pea had to poke around in the bin to rescue the invitations and made her run round all the houses posting them in double-quick time.

'Can't we just tell Tink we don't want to do the ex-merminating any more?' hissed Clover as they stumbled breathlessly back to the house.

But Pea shook her head firmly. Tinkerbell was happier than she'd been in months. Mum was too: Tinkerbell's sudden enthusiasm for all things Mermaid-flavoured had not gone unnoticed, and Mum was overheard telling Clem on the phone that Tinkerbell was settling into London life at last. Vitória – perhaps influenced by the sudden absence of peanut butter, jam or plastic bats from any of her possessions – was so impressed that there was even talk of introducing the Pot Noodle to the weekly Tesco shop.

'So long as Tink thinks we're ex-merminating, everyone's happy,' Pea told Clover. 'All we have to do is make sure none of her plans actually happen.'

But this was easier said than done. Pea would get off the school bus one stop early to put up posters, only to be informed the next day by a proud Tinkerbell that they had been spotted and spirited away. Meanwhile, as a treat for the bookshop customers, Vitória offered to make some of her favourite Brazilian sweets, *brigadeiro*, which were balls of chocolaty goop rolled in tiny strands of chocolate. Tinkerbell volunteered to help, and Pea had to watch her every move, to check that no razorblades or slug poison were 'accidentally' finding their way into the mixture.

'I wouldn't,' protested Tinkerbell afterwards. 'Brigadeiro's much too yummy to spoil. And we'll be the ones who get to eat it all, because no one's going to come to the book-signing, silly.'

Tinkerbell went back to the kitchen to suggest Vitória made another batch of fifty, just in case. Pea rushed to Mum's study, to print off an extra batch of invitations. The thought of Mum sitting alone in Sunflower Books with a giant pyramid of chocolate blobs before her was too distressing.

By the time Saturday came, Pea was exhausted with worry.

Clover, however, spent the morning getting Vitória to do one of her special twirly updos on both herself and Mum. Vitória offered to do Pea's in mouse-ear buns again, but Pea decided her usual ponytail was safer.

Vitória waved them off, and they set out across Queen's Park together, Wuffly included for moral support. It was a horribly windy day. By the time they arrived at Sunflower Books, Mum's and Clover's twirls were no longer twirly, and Mum looked nothing like the pretty, smoothed-out lady in the Marina Cove photos.

The tweedy-skirted Sunflower Books lady

didn't seem to mind. Her name was Jenny. She had glasses on a sparkly string round her neck, and was the sort of person who bent down to pat children on the cheek and say, 'Aren't you just darling?' without ever wanting to know their names, or if they liked being patted on the cheek. But she had put out a small table and piled it so high with *Mermaid Girls* books that Mum literally clapped her hands when she saw it, so Pea decided to like her anyway.

Pea Blu-Tacked pictures of Marina onto every available surface. Tinkerbell put brigadeiro all around the shop in little bowls, then stayed outside with Wuffly. Clover attempted to rescue Mum's hair.

'You have to look your best. And so do I, now I'm the daughter of a local celebrity,' she said. 'We'll probably start getting mobbed in the street soon.'

'Clover! Shush, you monstrous thing,' said Mum, and pointed out all the hundreds of books there were in the shop, all written by different people, none of whom were famous – not the way Clover meant – even though some of them had sold millions of books. 'Writers aren't film stars or superheroes. We're quite happy staying quietly in the background, letting our characters get all the attention, thank you. So don't go expecting a riot.' She tucked herself in behind the little table of books. 'If only a couple of people come and buy a book, I'll be more than happy.'

But it seemed as if even that might be ambitious.

One old man came in, looked at Mum's twirly hair, and walked straight back out again. A couple came in with a little boy in a pushchair, but they only wanted directions to the nearest Tube station. A woman bought some serious-looking hardbacks, and happily ate some brigadeiro while chatting to Mum, but she said she didn't have any children, and mermaids weren't really her thing.

'We are only a little independent bookshop,' said Jenny anxiously, looking at the one old lady who had come in during the last hour.

'You did post all those invitations, didn't you, girls?' said Mum, in a wilting voice.

'Of course we did,' Pea said hopelessly, while Tinkerbell grinned and gave her a thumbs-up through the window. The wind turned into heavy rain, which splattered against the window angrily, emptying the streets.

Tinkerbell and Wuffly came inside to stay dry.

Jenny made everyone cups of tea, just for something to do.

Pea sat in the children's section with a Jacqueline Wilson, *Double Act*; she'd read it before, but the familiarity was comforting – especially as she was finding it hard to concentrate on the words. She kept on picturing herself, very grown up and twirly-haired, sitting in a bookshop just like this one behind a stack of books by Pelagia Cove. *I wouldn't bother buying that*, said a loud man inside her head. *It's rubbish! Who ever heard of a mermaid called Beryl? And what kind of a name is Pelagia anyway?* And however hard she tried to fill up her imaginary shop with nicer people, the loud man seemed to scare them all away.

Then there was a rattle of the bell at the door, and suddenly the shop – the real one – filled up with chatter.

'Hello again!' said Mum. 'I wasn't expecting to see you here – how lovely!'

Pea shook herself back to reality, peered round a stack of picture books, and spotted Zhou and her mother – and more and more people, most of them Chinese, following her inside.

'Come in, come in,' said Jenny, collecting drippy umbrellas and offering the bowls of brigadeiro. 'Have chocolate! Buy a book! Please?'

'Zhou's such a fan, she just couldn't stay away,' said Zhou's mum, looking a little embarrassed. 'She talks about you so much at home, the rest of the family decided to come too. And these are some friends of Zhou's from Guides, and from school – you'll have met some of them already – and we seem to have picked up a few extras on the bus ride over. Hope you've got lots of ink in your pen!'

Within moments, the whole of Sunflower Books

was crammed with damp people, all talking about mermaids.

'See? Famous,' whispered Clover, a blissful look on her face.

Tinkerbell hid under Mum's signing table, sulking.

Pea stayed curled up in the children's section, peering over the top of her book to watch Mum transform into Marina Cove.

'Hello,' said a soft voice.

Pea looked up to find Zhou standing over her, wearing that same captivated expression of wonder.

'Oh! Um. Thank you for coming,' said Pea. 'And for bringing lots of people.'

Zhou smiled as if Marina Cove herself had said the words. Then she sat down beside Pea, pulled a tattered copy of the first *Mermaid Girls* book out of her pink backpack, and read while Mum finished book-signing.

Pea still couldn't concentrate on her Jacqueline Wilson. Mum had been right: she *had* made a friend!

She was Friendly (because she had brought lots of other friends with her – though she was choosing to sit with Pea). She was Unusual (because Pea hadn't met any Chinese people in Tenby, or Prestatyn, or Norway – though apparently there were quite a few in London). She was clearly Imaginative (because she liked Mum's books).

The rain cleared up, the empty brigadeiro bowls were collected, and people began to filter out of the shop. Mum was deep in conversation with Zhou's mum. Then she tiptoed over, knelt down, and said that Zhou and her mother were invited back to their house for cups of tea, to say thank you for bringing along so many people.

Zhou gasped.

Mum's eyes slid across to Pea, to check that was all right. Pea beamed back.

'Perfect!' said Mum. 'I do so like to meet my readers properly.'

'I know,' said Zhou. 'You adore the opportunity to see the dancing light of reading pleasure in a child's eyes, and regularly run Creative Writing workshops in schools and libraries.'

Mum blinked.

Pea did too: that was what it said on Mum's website, word for word. She'd written it herself, since Mum wasn't very good with technology.

'Mmmm,' said Mum, and hurried away to say goodbye to Jenny.

They set out together across the park, battling against the wind. Pea was worried that Tinkerbell's sulky face might put Zhou off being her new best friend. Then Vitória discovered they had un-expected guests, and banged the kitchen cupboards crossly as she started brewing the coffee.

But Zhou continued to be almost speechless with joy. She walked around the kitchen, touching things and whispering 'Marina's chair' and 'Marina's spoon' and 'Marina's old tissue' to herself. She squeaked when she spotted a printout of the first chapter of the new book, lying on the kitchen counter.

'Biggest fan,' said her mum, glancing apologetically at Mum.

'Why don't you two pop upstairs, Pea-hen?' said Mum, sweeping the new chapter out of sight. 'I'm sure Zhou would like to see your attic.'

Pea smiled gratefully and headed for the stairs, then realized that Zhou was not following. She was still in the kitchen, gazing, rapt, at Marina Cove hugging fresh pages to her chest. Mum had retreated behind a kitchen chair, as if she might need to fend her off like a lion-tamer.

Pea took Zhou's wrist, and gently pulled her up the stairs.

Zhou gave the attic exactly the sort of awestruck look Pea felt it deserved.

'So does your mum write in here? Does she type standing up? Is this the street she looks at while she's writing?' she said, peering out of the sloping attic window, fingers sliding reverently over the desk and the pencil tin.

'No,' said Pea, 'but I do.' She patted the pile of

notebooks on the shelf-desk, hoping to be asked about their contents. 'This is my room.'

Zhou looked around, wrinkling up her nose, then perched on the edge of Pea's bed. There wasn't really anywhere else to sit.

Pea sat quietly, not sure what to say. It was almost as if Zhou wanted to be best friends with Marina Cove, not Pea at all.

'Are those all your books?'

Pea relaxed. She could definitely make friends with someone who wanted to talk about books.

'Yep.'

'Have you read them all?'

'Yep.'

There was a long pause.

'Um,' said Pea. 'So. What books do you like?'

Zhou sighed fondly. She dug around in her pink backpack, and pulled out three *Mermaid Girls* books, all with the curly edges of love.

'I meant, apart from those ones.'

'Just these,' said Zhou, the reverence returning to her voice.

'Do you ever read books that aren't about mermaids?'

Zhou shook her head.

Pea didn't know what to say to that. She liked Mum's books a lot, but that didn't mean she wasn't allowed to like any others.

Zhou sucked her lip, her eyes travelling across the tiny room as if hoping Marina Cove might pop out of the wardrobe. They hit a small cardboard box with *Marinamail!* scrawled on the side, and lit up.

'Mum's fan mail,' explained Pea, opening the box up to show the small pile of envelopes within. She'd been so busy trying to keep an eye on Tinkerbell, they were still all sealed up.

'But why have *you* got them all?'

'I'm Mum's secretary,' Pea explained, relieved to be able to offer something of value. 'She's far too busy being authorial and important to read through all these letters, so I read them for her. Same with the online stuff – she gets lots of emails too.'

Zhou did not look as impressed as Pea had hoped.

'And the replies?' Zhou said in a small voice, picking up her much-crumpled copy of *Mermaid Girls 1: First Splash* again, and opening the back page to the photo of Marina Cove: *She gets letters from fans all over the world*, it read, *and she always replies personally to every single one.*

'Those are me too,' said Pea proudly. 'It takes ages, you know, because she gets *so many*. I tell her about the really best ones, obviously, if someone's written something really clever.'

(It wasn't completely true. After the first *Mermaid Girls* book came out, Marina Cove received precisely two pieces of fan mail. They had been pinned to the fridge with pride. Now, letters arrived in a slow but steady trickle, to the Dreaditor's office, where they were gathered up until there were enough to warrant a *Marinamail!* box.)

'It's all right, I can do her signature really well,'

said Pea. 'And I always draw a picture: a leaping fish, smiling, like the one on the book cover. Mum doesn't do that, but I think it looks more special that way. Look, I'll show you . . .'

But when Pea took the book from Zhou's hand and flipped to the front page, there it was already:

Hope you enjoy my book! May
mermaids swim beside you always,
Love Marina Cove

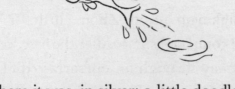

There it was, in silver: a little doodle of a fish. Pea's little doodle of a fish.

'Oh,' said Pea.

'I'd like to go home now,' said Zhou, picking up the book with two fingers and her mouth all puckered, as if it was one of Wuffly's post-park poo-bags.

'Coffee!' yelled Vitória from downstairs.

Mum made sure Zhou sat between Pea and herself. She offered milk and sugar, and asked Zhou boring questions about what subjects she liked best at school. But Zhou didn't say a word; just mournfully licked the strands off the outside of the last piece of brigadeiro.

As soon as her mother's cup was empty, she went straight to the front door and put on her coat.

'Can I sign a book for you before you go, sweetie?' said Mum, pulling out her special silver signing pen.

'No, thank you,' said Zhou curtly. 'I don't actually like your books.'

And halfway through an embarrassed 'Thank you' from her mum, the front door banged shut.

Mum put the radio on very loud as she loaded things into the dishwasher, but she didn't dance around the kitchen.

Pea concluded that the position of best friend was again open, and went upstairs, feeling quite sick.

That night she wrote a letter of resignation to Marina Cove, and left it at the study door on top of the *Marinamail!* box.

By morning it was gone, and Mum very kindly said no more about it.

Dear Mum,
I hereby resign from my position as secretary for Marina Cove. It is a bit like lying to have me signing your books for you (not that I am telling you off, because I know you are v busy and I liked doing it).
Love from Pea xx

PS You can copy my leaping fish if you like though.

CHAPTER 9

ELOISE

The weeks ticked by into October.

As Wuffly's daily walk became colder and muddier, Tinkerbell grew more gloomy – and more determined. Pea and Clover took to following her whenever she had a glass of fizzy pop in her hand, after the Great Keyboard Spillage made sparks fly out of Mum's computer. She was banned from using the phone, after the Dreaditor had called to say how sorry she was to hear about Mum's sudden phobia of water, and to ask, politely, if that really meant she was now allergic to mermaids. And when Pea and Clover failed to produce any new ex-merminating plans of their own, Tinkerbell took to shutting herself in her room to play Monopoly with Wuffly, even though Wuffly tended to eat the hotels.

Pea, meanwhile, had revised her 'Best Friend Requirements' list down and down until it contained only one item:

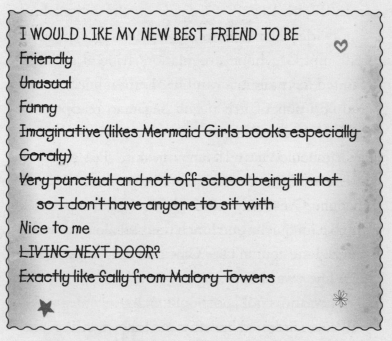

I WOULD LIKE MY NEW BEST FRIEND TO BE

~~Friendly~~

~~Unusual~~

~~Funny~~

~~Imaginative (likes Mermaid Girls books especially Coraly)~~

~~Very punctual and not off school being ill a lot so I don't have anyone to sit with~~

Nice to me

~~LIVING NEXT DOOR?~~

~~Exactly like Sally from Malory Towers~~

But in the company of Lilly, Elly and Molly, even

that seemed too much to ask. She resigned herself to friendlessness, and now sat alone at lunch times reading a book, while spooning her way through her food.

Clover, however, was beginning to unflatten. She took to humming the Pumpkin Carriage Overture from Tenby Royal's *Cinderella* on the school bus. She twirled her hair up into ribbons (green, blue, red – not Greyhope's regulation stripe at all), and painted her nails in a rainbow. Lemon juice, honey and odd pots of green goo began to reappear in the bathroom cabinet.

It should have been obvious, Pea realized afterwards. But it wasn't until she found herself spooning her way through a very soupy leek and bacon quiche one lunch time, all alone, that she realized she couldn't see Clover in the dining hall.

Clover was happy.

Clover was not at school lunch.

Pea abandoned her tray and followed the sound of jerky violins and shouting.

The music-room door had a sign with

DRAMA CLUB
Do Not Disturb
Creativity Happening

on it in purple scrolly writing.

Inside, Mrs Sharma, the drama teacher, was yawning, eating a banana and reading the newspaper with her feet up on the desk. She was even wearing slippers. Meanwhile Clover was on her feet, declaiming bits of *Hamlet* to a rapt audience of seven small Greyhope's girls.

'It was Dr Paget's idea,' explained Clover in a whisper, once she'd set the seven girls to try out declaiming to each other. 'In between *Moonlight Sonatas* I told her school was being a bit awful, and she said, "What one thing would make it better?" and I said, "Drama Club," only there wasn't one, and Dr Paget said that a capable girl like me shouldn't let a little thing like that stop me. She's so nice. Anyway,

Mrs Sharma said she'd be very happy to let me help her run a drama club – didn't you, Mrs Sharma?'

'Eh?' said Mrs Sharma, looking up from her paper. 'Yeah. Whatever you like, Clover love.'

'See? So here we are!' Clover beamed at her protégées as they took turns to cry, '. . . *the rest is silence,*' and noisily die of poisoning.

'I meant to tell you,' Clover added in a low voice, 'only I thought then Tink might find out. You can join too, if you like. You'll have to audition, though, because I made everyone else do it and it wouldn't be fair otherwise. You could do this bit of *Hamlet* – it's only drinking from a pretendy cup and falling over, really.'

But Pea shook her head. Mum had made her audition for *Cinderella* at the Tenby Royal when Clover did, because it would make things easier if they could go off to rehearsals together. All Pea could remember was standing at the edge of the enormous stage, with lots of lights shining in her eyes, while a man played the same beginning part of *The Sun'll Come Out Tomorrow* over and over again, waiting for her to start in the right place. They'd given up in the end. Mum had been very kind about it, and told everyone (Clover included) that Pea had a bad sore throat.

There weren't any lights or an enormous stage, but Pea didn't want to take the risk of opening her mouth and finding nothing would come out.

'No thanks, I'm a bit busy,' she said, and left.

She could hear them practising noisier deaths all down the corridor.

That night Pea finished her library book (*The Prince and the Pauper* – they were doing the Tudors in history, and she was trying to get ahead on who died and in what order), and went to poke through Mum's bookshelf in the study for another.

'Sorry!' she whispered when she found Mum at her desk in the dark, hunched over her computer and looking tired and dreary. 'Don't let me interrupt!'

But Mum stopped typing, and pulled Pea into a hug. 'Interrupting's very welcome,' she said. 'Some days it feels like I only ever talk to mermaids. And I always know what they're going to say, because I had to think of it first. Not fair at all.'

'I know what you mean,' said Pea feelingly. Her most interesting conversations all week had been in her head, pretending to swap clothes with Prince Edward. As she explained to Mum, he was a bit of a snotty character in the book, but at least fictional future kings didn't refuse to lend you their ruler in maths lessons.

Mum frowned, and moved a few papers around so there was room for Pea to sit down. 'We haven't had a proper chat in ages, just us, have we?' she said.

Pea shook her head. 'That's all right. I know you're busy – and I can always talk to Vitória.' She hoped that would make Mum feel better, but instead Mum's forehead went crumply.

They had a good long talk about London, and books, and exactly why she'd had time at lunch to read quite so many lately, even by her standards. Mum was very understanding, and got a bit sniffly exactly when Pea did, just so she wouldn't feel awkward. Then Mum tried to think of ways in which school – and lunch times especially – might be less miserable.

Pea went to school the next morning with a letter for the school secretary explaining that she would now have packed lunch, and a plastic box with leftover sweet-and-sour noodles in it. Greyhope's girls who had packed lunches didn't sit in the dining hall. If it was sunny there were picnic benches outside, or a grassy bit by the hockey pitches. If it was cold and wet (as it usually was), packed-lunch people went to their form rooms to eat at their desks. This was why afternoon lessons always smelled like orange peel, and sometimes you would open your history book and find a piece of lettuce in it.

FIVE FACTS ABOUT HENRY VII

Henry VII was a Welsh King (slice of tomato).

Henry VII was the first Tudor King.

Henry VII became King in 1485 after the Battle of Bosworth.

This was the end of the Wars of the Roses (splash of orange juice).

I only know 4 facts about Henry VII.

Pea was relieved to find only two girls in her form room: Eloise, who was tall, rather advanced in the chesty region and never seemed to do anything without tiny earbud headphones wedged into her ears; and Bethany, who had big feet and a keyring shaped like a pony.

Neither one of them was exactly the person Pea imagined as her new best friend. But they both looked harmless, at least. Eloise even smiled when she came in. There was definite Dot-replacement potential there.

'What have you got, then?' shouted Eloise, over the tinny pulsing of her headphones.

Pea took out her lunch box and showed her the pile of noodles inside. They'd gone a bit mushy since yesterday, but compared to Bethany's Marmite sandwiches and sat-on bag of Wotsits, they looked quite impressive.

'You can try some, if you like,' said Pea, offering her a rather sticky fork.

'No, thank you,' shouted Eloise, clicking the lid

off her own lunch box, which was bright red with lime-green latches to keep it shut. 'I'll stick with this.'

Pea wasn't sure *sandwich* was quite the right word for Eloise's lunch. It was some sort of extra-shiny bread woven in a knotty pattern, and it was so stuffed with layers of different kinds of cheese and strings of grated carrot and beetroot and frondy bits of posh leaves that Eloise had to squash it down really hard to take a bite.

She had lemonade too. The cloudy kind, in a glass bottle. With a straw.

'How were the noodles?' asked Vitória when Pea got home.

'Slithery,' she said, and told her about Eloise's sandwich in awestruck tones.

Vitória sniffed. 'Well, OK then,' she said. 'We will have to see what we will being doing about this, yeah? 'Cos I am not having one of my lunches made to look not very nice.'

But it was two days till the weekly big Tesco shop. The fridge contained half an onion and some sour cream. They were having a casserole for tea, which wouldn't be at all nice cold in a plastic tub the next day. Even the crusty endy bits in the bread-bin had vanished – traced to Tinkerbell, watching TV with telltale jam and crumbs all over Hannah Montana's knees.

'We're going to improvise, yeah?' said Vitória.

Pea went to school with a 'pizza bagel', which was really just a frozen pizza that had been attacked with pastry cutters so it was smaller and had a hole in the middle, and a chocolate finger wrapped in clingfilm. All the topping had slid off the pizza by lunch time, leaving a frayed white circle of pulpy white stuff with red slime smeared on it.

'That looks nice,' said Bethany, munching her Marmite sandwich solemnly, like a cow in a field of grass.

'It is,' said Pea, a bit optimistically.

Eloise's bright red lunch box was clicked open to reveal a glossy rice salad, with bits of ham and sesame seeds dotted all through it. There was a separate container too, for a perfect miniature fruit pie with a raspberry perched on top, and a single glistening profiterole.

'That looks nicer,' said Bethany, starting in on her sat-on packet of Wotsits.

'Thanks,' shouted Eloise sweetly, nodding her head to the whispery rhythm in her ears.

Pea tapped her foot along to the music, and thought hard about her old list of 'Best Friend Requirements'. Neither Eloise nor Bethany seemed to have a best friend already, and they hadn't been mean, or accused her of making up having a famous Mum – which counted as Friendly to Pea. She could definitely try making one of them her best friend. But which? Neither one of them seemed especially Funny, or Imaginative.

Nowhere had she included anything in her requirements about what her ideal best friend should have for lunch – but since neither girl talked all that much, it was the clincher. Squashed Wotsits were not anywhere near as appealing as miniature fruit pies. She wanted Eloise for a best friend.

'Mum!' Pea shouted when she got home from school. 'I think I'm making a friend! But I need earbud headphones. And an mp3 player. And definitely no more chocolate fingers wrapped in clingfilm.'

Mum – who had eaten a confusing lunch of pizza with a large hole in the middle – was unusually unsympathetic, and gave Pea a short lecture about girls who didn't have *any* chocolate fingers, ever, at all.

'I'll eat yours,' said Tinkerbell. 'I'd be grateful and everything.'

But Pea had eaten it already, which Mum said proved the point.

'But it's so we can be best friends!' said Pea, feeling cross now.

Tinkerbell gave her a furious look, muttered something about *serious* ex-merminators not needing best friends, and marched off to put on the TV as loud as it would go.

Vitória was much more understanding.

The weekly Tesco shop was brought forward.

Clover was recruited to offer sophisticated ingredient contributions.

Baby sweetcorn
Plover's eggs
Funny mushrooms
SUSHI!!! (yuck yuck yuck)

The next day, Pea's lunch was a ciabatta roll with cream cheese, baby tomatoes and rocket leaves. (Pea picked out the rocket leaves before eating it, because they were disgusting, but Clover said nasty lettuce was integral to the truly urbane sandwich.) There was also another chocolate finger wrapped in clingfilm (Mum had insisted) and an apple.

Eloise gave the roll an encouraging smile of recognition, before she opened the red box and took out a long furled tortilla wrap, bursting with babier tomatoes and rocketier leaves, which she didn't even pick out.

Pea was relieved to see that Eloise had an apple for afters too – but hers was chopped up in a little round pot. She wasn't sure why, but chopped-up apple seemed a million times better than one that was just round.

'But it will go all like brown on the edges and taste like mush, yeah?' said Vitória when she heard about the apple.

'I'll still eat it,' said Pea. 'I promise.'

But Vitória was right: the next day Pea found herself with a warm damp plastic box filled with warm damp brown-edged bits of apple. Eloise's little pudding pot was filled with fat green grapes, which didn't go mushy at all.

And so it went on.

Pea did her very best to compete. Vitória sat down with her over tiny cups of decaffeinated coffee when she came home each day, solemnly taking notes.

But every day Eloise seemed to have something new and different: tiny buns stuffed with turkey and cranberry sauce; little steamed dumplings with their own bottle of dipping sauce; meringues with golden stars painted on them in edible glitter.

When Mum did the housekeeping and saw the size of the Tesco bill, the lunch box project came to a stop. Competing with Eloise's lunch was just not compatible with being Well-Behaved.

Vitória was insulted, and sulked.

Pea had to admit she was relieved. After weeks of exhausting pre-lunch-time anxiety and racking her brains to find new things to put between two slices of bread, it was time to go back to having things in her lunch box that she actually liked – even if it meant that she would still be best friendless.

There was only one item on Pea's request list for the big weekly shop that week.

'Are you sure?' asked Vitória as they wheeled the trolley past the aisle full of anchovies and capers and other things that normal people picked off pizza.

It had been fun, spending all this time plotting menus with Vitória.

But Pea held firm.

Her lunch on Monday was an apple (unchopped) and a sandwich. Just an ordinary sandwich, on ordinary unshiny white sliced bread, with no fronds or grated strings of stuff; just a thick, even layer of chocolate hazelnut spread.

'That looks nice,' said Bethany.

Pea waited, resigned, for Eloise to take a bite from her chicken and bacon triple-decker flatbread, and Bethany to declare it nicer.

But Eloise had paused mid-bite. She stared. She lowered her sandwich. She *took out her headphones*.

'Is that chocolate spread?' she whispered, in rapt tones.

Pea nodded.

Eloise swallowed. She took another nibble of her triple-decker, but her eyes kept drifting longingly back to Pea.

Pea took a deep breath. This was it. She could eat her sandwich – or take a huge chance. She was

Lucy, stepping into the wardrobe, on her way to Narnia. She was Cedric Diggory, putting his name into the Goblet of Fire, even though there would be dragons to fight, and worse . . .

'Would you like half?' said Pea, holding out the lunch box.

'I'm not supposed to,' said Eloise, her voice suddenly very soft now she wasn't shouting over music. 'My dad runs a catering business – that's why I always have these stupid fancy lunches. But really I like chips and beans and stuff like that. And chocolate spread. Oooooohh, *chocolate spread.*'

Pea edged her lunch box even closer.

'If you really don't mind sharing . . .' said Eloise.

And she ate the half a sandwich in two bites, making ooohing noises throughout.

She even left the headphones out for the rest of lunch time. They talked about the hardness of French homework, and the horribleness of itchy stripy blazers. They shared the tiny lemon tarts

177

that Eloise had brought for pudding. Even Bethany tried one.

And that afternoon, Eloise sat in the empty chair beside Pea, all through history.

Pea was in heaven. She had all but given up hope of ever finding a new Dot, and now here was Eloise; chesty, grown-up-seeming Eloise, who doodled – in pen! – on her textbook, and wrote Pea distracting notes all through the lesson, like a real best friend.

At the end of the class, Ms Leonard announced they were to do special projects on Henry VIII, in pairs. Last week the prospect would've sent Pea into a panic. Now she had an instant project partner. (Eloise had her headphones in again when Ms Leonard had told them about it and hadn't heard a thing, but Pea felt that was the same as saying 'yes', really.) Pea picked 'Anne Boleyn' for them to work on together. It turned out you pronounced it like 'Anne Berlin', which was confusing, but she definitely sounded like Henry VIII's most interesting queen.

Pea almost danced through the front door that night.

'Well done you,' said Vitória, and painted Pea's stubby fingernails in a celebratory explosion of reds and purples.

Pea was so happy, she was genuinely disappointed when it came to half term, and there was no school for a week. All their plans had revolved around showing Clem the city, but after it was discovered that Mum had got the half-term dates wrong and Clem would not be coming to visit after all, Tinkerbell was so cross she turned the oven up on Vitória's carefully prepared Sunday roast, and ended up in such disgrace that all family fun was cancelled. Pea dedicated the week to making up for it – sorting out all the laundry into different colours, and ironing all Vitória's tiny vest tops, as a thank you for all her pre-chocolate-spread efforts.

After half term, lunch times became a new, stressless affair. Pea would bring her chocolate-spread sandwich, and swap half of it for whatever mysterious concoction Eloise found under the lime-green clips of her shiny red lunch box. Eloise would shout happily over the new track by The Uglies or Loud, Louder, Loudest that she'd downloaded that morning. (Pea never really understood who she was talking about, but Eloise didn't seem to mind.) Pea shared tales from home: about Mum's latest book idea, or the rope ladder made out of knotted-together socks she'd found in the laundry basket ('In case we needed to make a quick post-ex-mermination getaway,' Tinkerbell had explained nonchalantly). Eloise kept her headphones in, so Pea wasn't sure how much of it went in, but Bethany would nod along, chewing on her daily Marmite sandwich and her packet of Wotsits.

Pea felt sad for Bethany. Now that Pea and Eloise were best friends, Bethany was the left-out third one.

'Maybe you should try something different for

lunch one day,' Pea said to her, trying to be helpful and including.

It was a fateful error.

Bethany branched out into the world of portable yoghurt, which did not react well to being sat on, and exploded all over the inside of her school bag.

Eloise offered her a tissue to wipe the worst of it off *Junior Geometry 7*. 'That happened to me once, with a lemon soufflé,' she shouted sympathetically.

'I'll ask my sister – she might have a spare T-shirt,' said Pea as Bethany eyed her strawberry-yoghurty gym kit.

The three went off to look together. They found Clover in the drama classroom, being a Pirate King while the seven small girls climbed the rigging and swabbed the decks. Mrs Sharma was asleep on her desk, undisturbed by the buckling of swashes.

'Arrrr!' declared Clover, limping and squinting one eye shut in lieu of an eye-patch. 'What can I be doing for ye, me hearties?'

'Can Bethany borrow your gym kit? Only

we've got netball this afternoon, and hers is a bit yoghurty.'

'Arrrr! That ye can, young squire, if ye be asking for it in the true piratical way.'

Pea blinked. 'Um. *Please* can we borrow it?'

Clover tutted, petting an invisible parrot on her shoulder while she waited.

Bethany stared.

'Arrrrrr, Cap'n sir!' shouted Eloise, petting the invisible parrot too. 'Can we be borrowing yer PE kit is what yon Bethany means to say.'

Clover beamed, and clapped her on the shoulder. 'A likely lass ye are, me dear! Surely ye can. Take ye here this key to Davy Jones's Locker, and help yerself.'

She handed over the key to Bethany, then opened her squinty eye. 'It's not really Davy Jones's Locker, it's mine,' she whispered in her normal voice.

Then she squinted the eye back up and whirled round. 'Right then, you scurvy lot, which one of you salty dogs is going to walk the plank, eh?'

Pea and Bethany fled, and found the locker.

But Eloise didn't follow them.

Clover was flappy-armed with excitement on the bus home.

'Thank you so much for bringing your friend along!' she sighed. 'The others are all right at drowning and being marooned, but sometimes you need stabbing and marauding, and I can't do it all myself. Eloise got stuck in right away. *Very* impressive vocal projection.'

Pea smiled weakly.

The next day it was just her and Bethany for lunch, and she had her chocolate-spread sandwich all to herself.

'That looks nice,' said Bethany, solemnly munching her Marmite one.

Clover announced over dinner that her new Drama Club was doing *splendidly*, and that Mrs Sharma had asked her to arrange the Greyhope's Christmas play for the very end of term. There would be lunch-time rehearsals every day from now.

And that was that. Pea still saw Eloise in some of her lessons, and she had begun to take her headphones out more often – but all she ever talked about was how brilliant Pea's big sister was.

When Clover began taking chocolate-spread sandwiches to school for the Drama Club to share, Pea knew she had been utterly replaced.

'Don't be sad,' said Tinkerbell, finding Pea sitting on the bottom of her attic steps, trying to concentrate on Anne Boleyn. 'Not having any friends will give you more time to work on ex-merminating with me. Ooh, look! A torture chamber!'

Tinkerbell took *The Student's Guide to the Tower of London* out of Pea's hands, and began flipping happily through the pictures, her eyes lighting up at finding a chapter headed 'The Bloody Tower'.

Pea knew Tinkerbell was only trying to cheer her up, but 'not having any friends' kept ringing in her ears. If only Sam next door hadn't been so mean and cheesecake-stealing. She was prepared to give him or her a second chance, and had asked Clover if, on her visits next door, she ever saw Sam – but Clover was apparently always too busy drinking tea with Dr Paget and talking about plays, or herself. And anyway, there was never any waving from the other side of the wall. Only the occasional drifting of *Chopsticks* on the piano through the wall between the houses – a duet, to remind her that Sam, however horrible, had someone else to play with.

'Look, actual thumbscrews!' said Tinkerbell, holding up a gory picture. 'Those would definitely stop Marina Cove typing.'

'Tink!' Pea shook herself, pushing her best-friend worries aside. 'Listen – about the ex-merminating plan . . .'

Tinkerbell checked over both shoulders, then shot Pea a secretive grin. 'It's going brilliantly. Come and see,' she whispered, beckoning Pea downstairs.

'I wanted your help, but you've been busy with sandwiches so I had to do it all by myself.'

The *Marinamail!* box Pea had left for Mum weeks before had reappeared by the front door, ready to be collected and taken to the Dreaditor in the morning. Wuffly – who liked boxes – was sitting in it possessively.

'Shoo! You'll make all the replies smell like doggy bottom!' said Pea, sending her skittering away down the corridor.

Pea picked up the top few envelopes, to check them for hairiness. She couldn't resist peeking inside, to see what a *real* letter from Marina Cove was like.

It was not quite in the style she'd expected.

Dear Jennifer,
Thank you for your very kind letter. I would love to come to visit your school, but unfortunately I hate children of all ages, including my own. I suggest you take up

karate instead of reading. Never write to
me again.
Yours sincerely,
Marina Cove

Pea tried another.

Dear Princess Peach,
You have sent me a necklace made out of
lollipops. I am a 33-year-old woman. What
the hell am I supposed to do with this?

And a third.

Hi Tuuli,
The glitter in your letter went up my nose
and into my eyes and my brain and I am now
blind and in a coma. THANKS.

Pea got a sinking feeling.

There was a small pile of *Mermaid Girls* books

in the box too – all signed in twirly silver, with the authentically Pealike leaping fish. They said:

THAT WRITER YOU LIKE SO MUCH
MAKES ME SIGN THESE FOR HER
AND PAYS ME IN BISCUITS

Or:

Marina Cove isn't even a real person, you idiot.

And instead of 'Marina Cove', the squiggly signatures were made up of a selection of names taken from *My First Atlas*. (Vasco da Gama had, apparently, remarkably childlike handwriting.)

'Pretty clever, right?' said Tinkerbell, looking very proud of herself.

'No!' yelped Pea. 'You'll get Mum into loads of trouble!'

Tinkerbell rolled her eyes. 'Well, duh. Isn't that the whole idea?'

Clover heard the commotion, and carefully tugged the kitchen door shut so Mum wouldn't hear Pea's whispered explanation of what was in the *Marinamail!* box.

'Now, *Tinkerbell*,' Clover said, in a very passable impression of a disappointed parent. 'We can't *really* ex-merminate Marina Cove.'

'But you nose-promised!' Tinkerbell shouted in a thick voice, and barrelled upstairs, Wuffly bounding after her.

'Was she crying?' whispered Clover.

Pea thought she might have been.

Tinkerbell never cried; that had always been Clover's job. Pea felt terrible. It was the first time in her whole life that she'd broken a nose-promise. And though the ex-merminating plots had seemed like a game, it was obvious that for Tinkerbell it was all very real.

They went up to Tinkerbell's room at once, and fought their way past a very barky Wuffly.

Tinkerbell was sitting red-eyed and sniffly on

her bedroom floor, clutching *My First Atlas*. 'You're so mean,' she said miserably. 'Anyone would think you didn't *want* to get rid of the stinky *Mermaid Girls*.'

Clover and Pea curled up beside her.

'That's just it, Tink: we don't. I've got my Christmas play, and Pea's got her project. And there's Vitória. And Wuffly likes the park . . .'

'But you've still got an orange bedroom,' said Tinkerbell. 'And Pea hasn't got any friends. And you nose-promised!'

Clover sighed. 'I do. But it is a whole bedroom all to myself – I didn't have that before. And Pea will make some more friends. There's that Bethany I see you with sometimes, Pea; she seems nice enough.'

Pea's resolve faded for a moment. But this was bigger than just herself. She pictured the Dreaditor's face, stern and angry as she told Mum off about the *Marinamail!* box.

'Anyway,' she said firmly, 'you can't go writing evil letters to people who've read Mum's books. It's too much. Even for you.'

'You're just ganging up on me because I'm smallest!' shouted Tinkerbell.

'Well, maybe we are!' shouted Clover. 'No more ex-merminating, Tink. None. Or we'll tell Mum. *And* Clem. And you'll be in trouble for ever and ever.'

Pea was extra-glad she hadn't joined Drama Club. Clover could be quite scary when she tried.

Tinkerbell stuck out her bottom lip, sniffed, and nodded once.

They hid the box upstairs on top of Tinkerbell's wardrobe, before anyone could find it, and hoped the Dreaditor would think it had been lost in the post.

And nothing more was said about it.

CHAPTER 10

BETHANY VS. ANNE BOLEYN

A wet November turned into an icy cold December.

'Oh, kittens, I'm so pleased we're all happily Londonish Llewellyns at last,' said Mum, bundled up in three jumpers over Saturday breakfast at the café in Queen's Park.

It was true, mostly. Pea's weekly email to Clem had become much easier to write lately, now she didn't have to keep making up cheerful things to put in it.

Dear Clem,

How are you?

• Mum says for me to say hello and sorry again for not telling you the right dates for half term.

• Right now she is writing a chapter about a mermaid who suddenly grows green moss all over her face like a beard, and has to hide in a really big shell till she can think of a cure.

• She didn't tell me to tell you that bit, I just thought you might like to know.

• The Dreaditor says she has to finish this new book by Christmas Eve. Mum cried when she found out. We made her a bath with one of those exploding balls of fizzly grit in it to cheer her up. I think maybe that's where the idea for the moss came from actually. Don't buy the green kind of exploding grit balls for your bath is what I mean.

• Clover is going to be the Director of our school Christmas play. (Actually there isn't a

Director – Eloise said that Mrs King told Mrs Sharma that she had 'bloody well better organize something sharpish' and Clover has made herself a badge with DIRECTOR written on it.)

- Tinkerbell is fine.
- Vitória is fine.
- I have a new best friend called Bethany.

Hope you are well, we miss you, etc. etc.
Love from Pea (and everyone) xxxxx

Clover certainly seemed to have forgotten all about the woes of orange walls and insufficient shoes, now she had Drama Club. Choosing the Greyhope's Christmas play had been a challenge – but after several fruitless sessions of Clover sweetly asking for suggestions from the seven very small Year Sevens (while Mrs Sharma crunched her way through her lunch-time apple), Eloise had plucked Snow White and the Seven Dwarfs seemingly from nowhere. Lunch times and weekends were now busy with the hunt for stick-on beards, and the careful weighing up of whether Snow White or the Wicked Queen was the *real* main part.

Tinkerbell, to all appearances, was every bit as content. She had taken to spending long periods in her bedroom, 'inventing' something that required a screwdriver – though no one was allowed in to see it until it was finished. But even so, Pea could tell she was not quite herself. The weekly sighing letters from the head teacher complaining that Tinkerbell had been found in the wrong classroom, or on the roof, or on a Number 332 bus to Paddington, stopped entirely. It should have been comforting to know that she'd given up on ex-mermination, but the subdued, quiet Tink was somehow very sad to see.

But Pea was busy with worries of her own. She didn't like to seem ungrateful, but Bethany was not quite the best friend she had dreamed of. Still, it was good not to have to sit completely on her own at lunch (even if the conversation was limited to the niceness of her sandwich, and Pea talking on her own). Ms Leonard had agreed to let Bethany be her new partner for the Anne Boleyn project since Eloise kept being called out to play rehearsals, and Bethany tried hard, even if she didn't seem to care all that much about gluing things in straight. Pea had even been invited over to Bethany's house at the weekend, for a riding lesson.

Clover was thrilled on her behalf, and offered to pick her out a suitable outfit. Bethany lived in Hampstead, which Clover said was very 'ooh-la-la', and Pea couldn't possibly go horse-riding in saggy jog bottoms. Mum bonked Clover on the head with a packet of spaghetti, and said Pea should wear whatever would be comfy.

Pea wasn't sure she'd be comfy in anything, sitting on the back of a horse. Horses were high up, and bit people. She collected a pile of library books on Anne Boleyn and some Wotsits, in the hope of distracting Bethany from any mention of the riding lesson.

Vitória drove her to Hampstead (which *did* seem ooh-la-la, now Clover had said it, even though it was only streets and houses really), fretting all the way. Bethany was always so quiet and sandwichy. There might be long silences or hard questions, and parents to meet with no Mum or Clover around to charm them into liking her.

Vitória was very reassuring. 'You look nice! Very artistic. And even if this Bethany girl is, like, super fantastic horrible, you can just do the homework project thing and not talk, like in school, yeah? And if you don't want to go on the horse, you can just watch her going on it, right?'

Pea thought she could manage that.

But Bethany seemed entirely uninterested in Anne Boleyn, even after Pea explained the exciting parts like when she got her head cut off. All Bethany wanted to talk about was horses. Or ponies. Pea wasn't sure what the difference was, but there were an awful lot of posters of both, all over Bethany's bedroom walls. She wasn't in jog bottoms, either; she wore proper riding boots over leggings, and a hard plastic hat.

But the 'riding lesson' turned out not to involve a real pony at all – just Bethany holding the other end of a long ribbon while Pea ran around her in a circle, neighing reluctantly.

When Bethany offered her a sugar cube, to be eaten from the palm of her hand, Pea asked if she could use the phone and called Vitória to pick her up two hours early.

'Oh well. So you will probably not be being friends with this horsey girl from now on, yeah?' said Vitória.

Pea didn't know. After so long with no one to sit with at all, she wasn't sure horse-fondness was a sackable offence. Perhaps she ought to hang onto Bethany, at least till someone better came along.

At home Pea sat in the attic, and worked on the Anne Boleyn project alone. Anne was a very appealing sort of dead person, if the library books were right. She was Henry VIII's second queen, which was, apparently, a shocking thing to be in those days and caused wars and made the whole country change religion. She was famously witty and intelligent. She loved books, dancing and art. She also always wore a necklace with the letter 'B' on it, which Pea envied (Vitória had a letter necklace too: a small 'V' with sparkly diamanté spots all over it), and was very beautiful (or had a huge thing like a tumour growing out of her neck, depending on which book you read; Pea preferred the version without). It was a shame, Pea thought, that she was dead – she would've made an excellent best friend.

I WOULD LIKE MY NEW BEST FRIEND TO BE
Friendly <– Bethany
Unusual <– Anne Boleyn – a) dead b) a queen
Funny <– Anne Boleyn – made the whole French court laugh

Intelligent <- Anne Boleyn – Bethany got a D in French, Anne Boleyn spoke it perfectly

Very punctual and not off school being ill a lot so I don't have anyone to sit with <- Bethany

Nice to me <- Anne Boleyn (does not try to groom me, has never called me Pebbles and told me to canter, etc.)

POINTS: Bethany 2, Anne Boleyn 4

'You are creepy and weird,' said Tinkerbell.

I didn't mean to be, Pea thought, but it was possible.

At school, Bethany sat beside her, contented and oblivious.

'You can't come to my house this weekend – we've got painters coming,' said Bethany in between bites of Marmite sandwich.

'That's a shame,' lied Pea.

'I'll come to your house instead,' said Bethany.

'Oh,' said Pea. 'Will we do riding lessons again?'

'Of course,' said Bethany seriously. 'We haven't done jumps yet.'

Pea developed a picture in her mind of herself leaping feebly around the garden over a series of small fences, Bethany trotting behind her shouting, '*Clip-clop, horsey! Clip-clop!*' while Clover, Tinkerbell, and even floppy-haired Sam from next door watched with their mouths open.

When Ms Leonard announced that the whole of Pea's history class would be going on a trip to the Tower of London that Friday, however, Pea reflected that Bethany had one fundamental virtue: Anne Boleyn would be no use at all when it came to having someone to sit next to on the coach.

'You jam tart, you! Can I come?' said Mum when she signed the permission form for the trip. 'We never got to go anywhere as swish as the Tower of London when I was at school. It was the local aquarium or nothing, and that wasn't even an aquarium really; more a big tank full of those ugly flat fish.'

'I suppose you could come,' said Pea doubtfully, wondering how to ask Ms Leonard – but Mum laughed and said she was only joking.

'Don't think the Dreaditor would be too impressed if she found out I was bunking off,' she said. 'Anyway, Friday's one of my school visit days. Can't miss that.'

Pea went to Tinkerbell's room to take back her *Student's Guide to the Tower of London* (Tink wasn't there, which Pea thought was odd; she was sure no one had gone out again after school) and read it three times, cover to cover. This was the place Anne Boleyn herself had been imprisoned by Henry VIII. The thought of going into the real room where she had lived, the actual spot where she had met her death, was a total thrill. Perhaps seeing that would help Bethany to understand Anne's charms.

But at Tuesday lunch time Pea came back from

the toilets to find Bethany holding Pea's best silver-starred notebook, open at the 'Best Friend' voting scores.

'I only made you be a pretend pony because we can't afford a real one,' said Bethany, her face quite beetrooty. 'And if you didn't want to be friends, you could've just said.'

Pea felt terrible. She remembered how full of hope she'd been about meeting floppy-haired Sam next door, and how awful it had felt when she – or he; she still had no idea – had turned out to be so nasty. What Pea had done was even worse: it wasn't very nice for poor Bethany to find herself coming second best to someone who'd been dead for almost five hundred years.

She *had* become a new London Pea; a selfish one who stayed friends with someone she didn't like all that much, just so she wouldn't feel so alone. Clover, and even Tinkerbell, had settled down to London life. Only Pea had failed. All she had wanted to do, ever since they arrived, was make a new best friend – and now she wasn't sure she even deserved one.

Bethany moved seats in all their lessons, and ate her lunch on a picnic table outside, shivering, rain pouring off her anorak hood straight into her Wotsit packet, and Pea couldn't blame her at all.

Ms Leonard refused to let her switch projects. Pea wondered if anyone at Greyhope's would mind if she just sat in the school library on Friday, instead of going on the trip – but Ms Leonard gave them a reminding lecture about how awful it would be if anyone missed it, how ruinous it would be to the class project, how cripplingly sad it would make her if someone arrived even five minutes late. She and Bethany would have to spend all Friday at the Tower of London side by side.

There was only one thing for it.

'I don't feel very well,' Pea said on Thursday night.

She waited for the chorus of concern, but

Vitória just said, 'What a pity,' and carried on eating her bowl of Coco Pops, and Mum didn't say anything at all.

'No, but *really*,' insisted Pea, and pressed Mum's hand against her forehead. 'I'm all hot and feverish.'

She was too: she'd been lying with her face against the radiator for twelve whole minutes.

'Feels all right to me, chicklet,' said Mum, and shooed her upstairs.

Pea sat on her bed feeling very cross and grotty, trying to think diseased thoughts. It was difficult, trying to convince herself into a headache. But the more anxious she felt about the next day, the more grotty she felt. It was quite impossible to eat any dinner. By the time she went to bed, there really *was* a headache.

By morning, Pea was in a fog. Her legs were heavy. Her throat hurt. Her ears felt stuffed with tissues, and when she stood up, it was as if someone was standing on the top of her head, willing her to lie back down.

'Oh, Pea-pod,' said Mum, 'I'm sorry, I thought you were just having a whinge – but you really are poorly!'

Pea thought dimly that she hadn't meant to be, not really. But Mum stuck the beepy thermometer under her arm and it read 39.9, which was apparently very warm indeed. Mum rang Greyhope's at once, and told them that Pea was much too ill to go on the Tower of London trip.

'But what am I going to do with you?' wailed Mum. 'I can't leave you here – Vitória's got the day off and she left for Canterbury hours ago. And I can't cancel my school visit, not at such short notice. Oh, if only Clem was a bit closer . . . or *anyone* . . . Oh, I knew this would happen . . .'

'Don't panic,' said Clover, arriving with a cool glass of water that was meant for Pea, but which Mum suddenly seemed to need most. 'She can go next door for the day. Dr Paget can look after her.'

Pea didn't like the sound of that.

Mum clearly didn't either. 'Are you sure? I don't like to ask . . . We've never really . . .'

But Clover skipped between the houses, and was back in no time.

'It's all arranged,' she said. 'Dr Paget says she doesn't mind one bit, but we should bring a bucket if she's the sicky sort of ill.'

Pea hadn't thought she was, until there was mention of buckets. She went green on the way down the stairs, and had to have a sit down. They wrapped her in a duvet before going outside, and the chilly air on her face made her feel a little better.

Then she was lying on the plush golden sofa with a washing-up bowl on the carpet beside her, feeling very green again, while Dr Paget smiled and gently patted her hair.

'Mum?' said Pea in a small voice.

'She'll be back later,' said Dr Paget. 'I've got clients in the kitchen, but you can ring the bell if you need something.'

She held up a small brass bell and jingled it.

Pea thought Dr Paget wasn't at all the sort of person you should summon by jingling a bell, and fervently hoped she wouldn't need to. Then she was sick in the washing-up bowl. It turned out Dr Paget was the sort of person who was very sensible and unbothered about sicky people, which helped.

It was a very odd sort of day.

Pea dozed. Sometimes she was awake enough to wonder if she might not be ill at all in the usual sense, and if a medical doctor came to take her temperature she would say, *Aha! This young lady has a case of Convincer's Syndrome, common among schoolgirls who are worried about going on trips*. Other times, her head was so spinny and fuzzy that when Sam came home from school at lunch time, she was sure she could see *two* Sams – one offering a glass of water, one a slice of dry toast.

She slept and slept, and eventually woke up enough to realize that it was dark outside, and the voices she could hear from the kitchen weren't 'clients' but Mum talking to Dr Paget.

'Vitória's good company,' Mum was saying in a quavery voice. 'And the girls keep me entertained, of course. It hasn't been easy for them, all these years, and I so wanted to give them a proper home; somewhere we'd stay till they were grown.'

'But . . .' said Dr Paget gently.

Mum started to say something, only it disappeared into a sort of wobbly noise.

Pea sat up.

'It's just . . . lonely,' said the wobbly voice, neither Marina-ish nor Mumlike. 'I don't think I'd realized how settled I'd got in our last place, and then this morning, when I realized there was no one to call who could just pop in and help out . . . the sort of people who are just around, always . . . And with my work now, I don't meet people, not the way I used to. Not to get to know them. Not *friends*.'

Pea tugged the duvet tightly around herself. All this time she'd been desperately hunting for a new best friend – and had no idea that a mum might need a Dot-like person too.

Then Dr Paget started saying all sorts of things about Dr Skidelsky being away all the time, and how she spent days sometimes only listening to other people's problems and no one remembered to ask her if she was all right, and how lovely it would be to have someone next door to moan at about the postman or politics or an unfortunate haircutting decision – and for nice things too, like going to the cinema. So apparently a Dr Paget needed a Dot too.

It was a disappointment, finding out that adulthood didn't fix that sort of worry all by itself. But then Mum and Dr Paget started talking about films they'd wanted to see but forgotten to, and books everyone else seemed to have read, and the terrifyingly addictive lure of *Homes under the Hammer*, and Pea knew it would be all right.

'Are you feeling better?' said a voice.

It was Sam.

Pea took in the green stripy hoodie and jeans, and the floppy hair, and still had no idea if it was a boy or girl or why it suddenly cared whether she was better or not, but she was too tired to be disagreeable.

'I'm glad you're here,' said Sam, sitting on the end of the golden sofa. 'Not glad you're all green, obviously. But I missed it when you stopped waving. I threw more footballs over with messages in, but you never replied, and Sam said I was being pathetic, so I stopped.'

Pea blinked, feeling ill again. '*Sam* said that?' she said.

'Yes,' said Sam. 'Not me, obviously. The other Sam. You know we're twins, right?'

As if to prove it, another Sam appeared in the doorway – this one wearing a red stripy hoodie and jeans.

'Ha!' said the Sam in the red hoodie. 'Look at her! Not a clue. As if we're at all alike. We're not even identical!'

Now that there were two of them in the same place, Pea could see there were plenty of differences between the two Sams. Sam on the sofa, in the green hoodie – his name was Samuel, apparently – had a narrower face. Sam in the doorway, in the red hoodie – Samantha – was a fraction taller, and more freckly. But if they weren't together, she would never have been able to tell them apart.

'So it was Samuel who wanted to be my friend,' said Pea slowly, 'and Samantha who ate all the cheesecake, and lied about the dog.'

'Duh,' said the Sam in the red hoodie.

'Only our mums say you can't call us that,' said the Sam in the green hoodie. 'We're both just Sam, always.'

It turned out Dr Skidelsky was writing a very important book about the difference it made to call someone a 'boy' or a 'girl' name when they were growing up, and the two Sams were her biggest piece of research.

'My mum puts us in her books too,' said Pea sympathetically. 'And my character *died*.'

Sam – green hoodie Sam – widened his eyes, alarmed.

Sam – red hoodie Sam – laughed. Lots.

Pea, conscious that they would at some point change their clothes, mentally named them Sam One and Sam Two, and hoped Dr Skidelsky wouldn't put that in her book.

Once it was confirmed that, yes, Pea was feeling much better, thank you, Mum (looking a little red-eyed, but smiling) said it was time they let the Paget-Skidelskys get back to normal. Pea gathered the duvet around herself, and promised to introduce Sam One (the nice one) to Wuffly when she was completely well again. Mum, meanwhile, gave Dr Paget a very tight hug, called her Genevieve, said she couldn't thank her enough and promised, several times, that they would do lunch. They stood chatting on the doorstep so long that Pea's teeth began to chatter, and she had to be hurried away down the drive at speed before she could have a relapse.

'Just think,' said Clover, emerging from her mountain of important Directorial script notes. 'There really was a best friend next door, waiting for you all this time.'

Pea smiled.

Mum smiled too, her eyes shining.

Pea hugged the duvet around herself on their own sofa, and went back to sleep.

And that was that.

Mum had a Genevieve to eat lunch with; Clover had her dwarfs; and Pea had a Sam One. Vitória took up pilates and a bedtime routine of universal hot chocolate, and it would soon be Christmas.

All was well, except for Tinkerbell.

THE TOWER
OF LONDON

December whizzed by in a whirl of messages-in-footballs, poisoned apples, and frantic mermaid avoidance.

Sam One turned out to be an excellent best friend, even though he was a boy, and didn't go to Pea's school. As soon as she was feeling better, he came to their house, and together they braved the cold to uncover a hidden cache of ripped footballs and old plastic water bottles, wedged down the back of the shed, containing increasingly plaintive old messages.

215

Dear Pea,
I'm sorry I didn't get to meet you. You could come over again and not hang on the monkey bars, if you don't like monkey bars.
From Sam

Dear Pea,
I am here all day today, if you wanted to come over today.
From Sam

Dear Pea,
We have orange juice (without any bits in). In case you like orange juice.
From Sam (the one who lives next door)

'I can't believe these were here all along!' said Pea. 'And that every single one of them fell down the back of the shed.'

'Highly suspicious,' said Sam One seriously.

Tinkerbell (who was hovering on the patio with Wuffly, watching them) put on her most innocent face, and went inside immediately.

'Oh no! Tink, you didn't!' Pea shouted after her.

But Sam One shrugged it off. ''S all right. It's the sort of thing Sam would do.'

Pea thought that eating most of a cheesecake and pretending a dog had stolen it was the sort of thing Tinkerbell would do too – but when Sam said that her idea to throw a message in a football had been 'ingenious', Pea forgot all about it.

'So what is it like, Sam, to be having two mums?' said Vitória, making them hot chocolate in her tiny coffee cups. 'Do kids say horrible mean things at your school? Is they both called "Mum"? Because already in your house there is two Sams, so this is, like, well confusing.'

Pea was glad Vitória didn't mind being nosy; she was very curious to know too, but not sure it was polite to ask.

Sam didn't mind. The answers were: 'Just

ordinary'; 'Not for ages'; and 'Mum K and Mum Gen.' In return, he wanted to know what it was like for Pea to have *two* sisters, and a mysterious missing pirate dad, and to live with one mum and a Vitória – and he seemed to think that was every bit as unusual.

Really, Pea thought, there was no such thing as a normal family; just yours, and everyone else's.

Dear Diary,

Today me and Sam One started writing a story together about a superhero with webbed feet and laser eyes (his idea) called Anne Boleyn (my idea). I am doing the words and he is doing the pictures as he is really good at drawing.

When it's finished we're going to show it to the Dreaditor, and maybe she can make it a real proper book.

I love having a best friend! Even though Sam

One isn't at all like Sally from Malory Towers, or lots of the things on my list.

I think maybe having a 'Best Friend Requirements' list isn't the best way to find a best friend. People aren't very list-like.

Clover, meanwhile, had resolved her casting dilemma. Eloise was playing Snow White, and Clover the Wicked Queen (who had two costume changes, a lot of running to stand behind the mirror to be her own reflection, and absolutely zero lying around being asleep for half the story, so it was definitely the best part). Finding a Prince Charming and a Huntsman had proved more difficult. Fortunately Molly – the round one with the red glasses from Pea's class – had fallen out with Lilly and Elly after wearing the wrong sort of socks, and Clover had found her wandering the halls one lunch time as if seeking a sleeping lady in a forest. And Pea, still feeling terrible about the

219

notebook, pleaded with Bethany to stop shivering outside at lunch times, and to at least come into the warm to watch the rehearsals. Clover recruited her at once. Bethany still wasn't talking to Pea, but Clover said she was remarkably good with a prop axe, and that was comfort enough.

Mrs Sharma had sold tickets. Mrs King had been instructed to stop fussing about Clover's undone homework. Rehearsals were still rather chaotic, and the Art Club's efforts at building a glass coffin had been sent back several times with notes (*More glassy! More coffiny!*), but according to Clover, it was going to be amazing.

Mum was busy too. She saw Dr Paget for coffee or sandwiches most days. Sometimes Dr Skidelsky came too, if she was in London. She joined Dr Paget's book club, which seemed to be more of a cheese-eating club when it was her turn to host ('And six bottles of wine!' said Clover. 'Six!'), and went to the small local cinema to watch glum foreign films which all seemed to be about people killing themselves, or each other, and crying about it.

The one thing Mum was not doing was writing. The next book was supposed to be done and delivered to the Dreaditor by Christmas Eve. But she had stopped talking excitedly about underwater fire-caves and furry green mermaids, Pea noticed, and when Pea went to write Clem's weekly email on the computer, it wasn't even switched on.

It seemed ex-mermination was happening without Tinkerbell needing to use *My First Atlas* at all. Pea would've been suspicious, but Tinkerbell truly did seem to have given up her campaign. She was still subdued and quiet, spending longer and longer periods tucked away in her bedroom, so focused on her mysterious 'invention' that she refused to answer the door when Pea knocked.

'Maybe your mum's got Writer's Block,' said Sam One seriously, as they watched her bundling herself up in a hat and coat to take Wuffly out for a third walk that morning.

Pea shook her head. 'Mum says it doesn't exist.'

'Maybe she's just never had it before.'

Pea supposed it was possible. She herself had never had any trouble thinking of new ideas – finishing one story before a new, shiny, more enticing one arrived in her imagination was much more of a problem – but after four *Mermaid Girls* books, perhaps Mum was finding it hard to feel creatively excited.

'We need to inspire her,' said Pea, with determination.

Sam One hurried next door to fetch a CD of whale noises that Dr Paget sometimes used with patients. Pea dashed around the house, collecting Inspiring Objects to put in Mum's study: a jam jar of water with blue food colouring in it (so it would look oceany); windchimes; one of Pea's own notebooks and a pencil.

Clover had a pearly seashell in her room which would be perfect too, but when Pea and Sam One knocked, she shouted, 'I'm learning my lines!' in her most fearsome Wicked Queen voice, and slammed the bedroom door so hard the scrolly-written *Director at Work* sign fell off.

They could make do without.

Sam One put the whale noises on extra loud. Pea laid the tray with the Special Writing Tea on it, ready for when Mum came back from her walk. But Mum just ate the Twix and left the computer off.

As Christmas drew closer, it got worse.

Christmases in the Llewellyn household were enthusiastic, at minimum. When you moved around so much, you bumped into quite different ways of doing things. In Amsterdam Clover and Pea had joined in making *Sinterklaas* biscuits on December 5th, put out shoes by the fire (on the windowsill, really, since there wasn't one), and woke up to find an orange in the left and a *speculaas* biscuit in the right. On the houseboat in Norway, Pea wore a white dress and a hat made of pine cones on the 13th, and they ate *pinnekjøtt* and mashed-up turnips on Christmas Eve while waiting for Julenissen to bring marzipan. Madagascar (according to Clover;

that was BP as well as BT) was much like Prestatyn, with robins and snow on cards and a big friendly lunch – except it was boiling hot when people wished each other '*Mirary Krismasy*' and the lunch was rice, not turkey.

By the time Tinkerbell was born, they had collected so many traditions that when the 25th arrived, it felt like the gloomy end of a very long party. It was not easy finding *speculaas* or salted lamb and birch branches for cooking your *pinnekjøtt* in Tenby either, and there were Well-Behaved times when even buying one round of chocolate Father Christmases meant soup for lunch and toast for tea for a month. Mum had, eventually, put her foot down.

Nowadays there were only two absolute requirements of a Llewellyn Christmas: that they should go open-air swimming before breakfast (Mum had said it one year, sleepily, when Clover and Pea had woken her up at 4 a.m., insisting it was daytime: 'Go and jump in the canal,' she'd mumbled, and they did, because at Christmas improbable things from grown-ups suddenly became quite usual); and that there were bacon sandwiches for breakfast. That had been Clem's contribution. It went well with the swimming, so they kept it.

But Pea worried that she was the only one in the family who had remembered – and she had no idea how they were going to find somewhere to go swimming, now they were so far from the sea.

There was a pool down the road, but it had a severe CLOSED UNTIL NEW YEAR notice up already, and she didn't much fancy the duckpond in Queen's Park. (Wuffly had weed in it at least twice.)

'Maybe you could all jump in the Thames?' Sam One suggested.

But they looked it up at the library, and discovered that it was full of dangerous currents, and mudbanks that would suck you in, and you might get hit by a passing boat.

'But we *have* to find somewhere!' Pea said. 'It's traditional!'

She hoped Clover might have a suggestion, but the Wicked Queen shouted, 'Leave me alone, I'm sticking on my warts!' and slammed the bathroom door in her face.

Tinkerbell glared so fiercely whenever the subject of Christmas was raised that Pea didn't like to ask.

And Mum was hopelessly vague on the subject. 'Oh, I expect we'll come up with some sort of planlet, my mermaid. Don't you worry about it,' she said.

'But is there bacon on the shopping list? And you do know my swimming costume doesn't fit any more? And is Clem coming to stay?'

Tinkerbell glared even more fiercely at that.

Mum was unmoved, and maybe even slightly cross. 'Don't flap, Pea. It'll all get sorted – but I can't be too distracted by festive things right now: you know I've got a deadline.'

But they went to four different shops before Mum could pick a Christmas tree – a two-metre

Colorado Blue Spruce – and then it took all afternoon to find lights that she liked. The girls came back from school one day to find that Mum had evidently devoted it to winding tinsel around the balusters, the picture frames, even the light switches in every room in the house. It looked very Christmassy, but it wasn't going to get Mum's book finished, or find them a swimming pool.

Vitória was no help: she was forever fussing about with flight times back to Brazil for the holidays, and got anticipatorily weepy at the mention of family Christmases.

Pea sent an emergency email to Clem, but that was no help either.

Hi P,
Sorry, love, don't stress, ask your mum.
C

The house next door was no respite. Instead of *Chopsticks*, Pea could often hear *Jingle Bells* plinking through the wall. Dr Paget, to Pea's surprise, adored Christmas and had taken to wearing a woolly jumper with reindeers knitted into it – much to Dr Skidelsky's disgust, as she called it 'an appalling pageant of consumerism', and wouldn't even eat turkey on principle.

Pea hoped she never had the sort of principles that involved not eating turkey.

When Dr Skidelsky was in Edinburgh, however, Dr Paget filled the place with her version of Christmassiness – all cloves and oranges and cinnamon sticks, and tiny gift boxes wrapped in brown paper. Her Christmas tree was a branch from the garden, with handmade paper crackers tucked among the twigs. There were no glitzy gaudy baubles either; the only decorations were hand-drawn ones, tied on with hairy gold string.

'One for each of us,' explained Sam One, showing her the pencil sketch of himself (which Pea thought was a very good likeness; he'd got the narrowness of his face down perfectly). There was one for Sam Two, Dr Paget (she'd signed it Genevieve), and even Dr Skidelsky (signed Kara, in Sam One's writing, and the picture was his too: a cross round face, its eyes looking up disgustedly at the Santa hat perched on its head).

Pea loved the idea. Mum had already loaded the two-metre Colorado Blue Spruce's branches with more tinsel and dangly things than was quite sensible, but she loved the idea too, and another writing afternoon was lost in cutting and sticking.

Mum made hers with two sides – one Mum, one Marina, complete with fishy tail. Pea wished she'd thought of doing that herself, but she had to make Clover's too (the Director was otherwise occupied, phoning up dwarfs and shouting, 'I don't care if you've got a violin exam tomorrow, this is *theatre*!'). Tinkerbell seemed to take for ever over hers, and to use up every fleck of glitter in the house – but it turned out she was making one for Clem, not herself.

'Oh, Tink,' said Mum, smiling awkwardly. 'That's – it's – that's very nice of you. He'd really like it.'

Tinkerbell made another one for Wuffly. Mum drew Tinkerbell's. Pea made one for Vitória.

'There,' said Tinkerbell, hanging them up one by one. 'Now all the family is on the tree.'

Vitória looked at hers, and burst into tears. (Mum promised it was nothing to do with Pea's drawing, which had come out with more teeth and bigger ears than was quite kind; just that Vitória was feeling a little bit homesick.)

That was the trouble with Christmas, Pea thought. It mattered that it was right; almost too much.

December 21st rolled around. The day of Clover's play; the last day of school; three days before Marina Cove was meant to have finished her book; and four till Christmas.

It snowed.

Big, proper snow, with fat blobs of snowflakes

all stuck together at first, and then a solid blizzard that built a drift outside the front door within half an hour.

Vitória was mesmerized. It was her first snow. Apparently in Recife it rained a lot, especially in the winter (which was the same time as summer in London), but never got much cooler than a warm summery day. She went and stood in the street in her yellow dressing gown and Mum's tall boots with her arms out, until her face got so cold it made her weepy again.

Pea understood. It had hardly ever snowed in Tenby either. It had, once, in Prestatyn (that was the day Mum had decided not to live in the yurt any more), and the houseboat in Norway was frozen in quite regularly, which was mostly a bit cold and horrible and made big spiders come out of the lockers above her bed. But London snow, especially just before Christmas, was a special thrill.

'It's a disaster,' moped Clover into her cereal bowl. 'Every director's nightmare!'

'Shush, you misery,' said Mum, who was on the phone to the school. 'Hmm. The machine says the school is open, but not all the teachers will be able to make it in, and to only come if you can be sure of making it home again.' She peered at the softly falling snow outside. 'I declare a snow day!'

'Nooooo!' wailed Clover. 'We've got the dress rehearsal all afternoon! I *have* to be there! People are counting on me, Mother!'

Mum suggested that perhaps Clover had been spending a little too long in character as the Wicked Queen lately, and taking the day off would help her to save something for the big performance that evening (which, she added quickly, was sure to go ahead).

'It'll probably stop soon. We don't want to waste it.'

'Shouldn't you be writing, though?' said Pea.

'Blah to writing! Poo to Chapter Twenty-three! I can't be expected to work when no one else is!'

Pea wasn't sure the Dreaditor would see it that

way – she seemed the type who would get to the office regardless; the snowdrifts probably hurried out of her path all by themselves – but Mum was adamant.

'Come on, my squishies! Wrap up warm, we're going out.'

'Where?' said Clover.

'Where do you want to go?'

'Can we go to the Tower of London?' said Tinkerbell.

Mum paused, blinked, then shrugged. 'Yeah, why not?'

'Really?' said Pea.

Tinkerbell patted Pea's hand. 'I know you missed your school trip because you were all pukey and disgusting. But I'd like to go too. I'm totally interested in history now. And it'll be better all covered in snow, because everything is.'

Pea was mildly suspicious, but she remembered Tinkerbell reading her *Student's Guide to the Tower of London*, especially the chapter about the Bloody

Tower. It did sound like the sort of thing Tinkerbell would like.

'Can Sam One come too?' asked Pea. 'Or will it cost too much money?' She knew the tickets weren't cheap. They were meant to be being Well-Behaved still, *and* it was just before Christmas.

'The more the merrier!' said Mum. 'Sam Two can come too.'

'No!' said Tinkerbell, her chin shooting up. 'Sam Two can definitely not come!'

Pea stared at Tinkerbell. Sam Two wasn't Pea's favourite person either, but she didn't think Tinkerbell cared that much.

'She blamed Wuffly for eating the cheesecake,' mumbled Tinkerbell eventually, after much prodding.

'Be fair, Tink – we can't invite one and not the other,' said Mum, and phoned Dr Paget. It took her a few tries to get through, while they all went off to put on three layers of socks and woolly tights under their jeans.

It turned out that Sam Two was showing signs of coming down with a bug – perhaps the same poorliness that Pea had had. Dr Paget was worried that meant Sam One could be getting it too, and might suddenly need to be sick in a washing-up bowl while they were out – but Mum was comfortingly untroubled, and said that in that case Clover and Tinkerbell and even herself might too, and if that happened they could all be sick together, but it seemed a shame not to go.

Vitória was invited, but declared it 'like, very freezing and everything, yeah', and set herself up for a day beside the radiator.

By nine o'clock they were on the Tube.

It was a long journey: Jubilee Line to Baker Street (in a carriage that started off friendly and full of pink-faced, happy people in snow-frosted woolly hats, and slowly got hotter and crosser as it got more tightly packed with commuters), then a mad chase through white-tiled tunnels onto the Circle Line, which was grubbier but almost empty once everyone else got off at Euston Square, so they could sit down.

Pea showed Sam One *The Student's Guide*, with the painting of Henry VIII on the cover. Sam One said he'd been to visit it once before, years ago, so he knew lots already – especially the torturing and putting heads on spikes at Traitors' Gate. That kept Tinkerbell entertained for the rest of the trip.

The Tower of London turned out not to be a tower at all; not just one, anyway. It was like several storybook castles at once: the White Tower in the middle, and then all around it high walls with arrow-slits and more round towers, running along the edge of the Thames. Tinkerbell had been right: it did look very grand all frosted with white, through a curtain of whirling flakes.

They shivered in the snow as Mum queued for tickets, then they crossed over a drawbridge and wandered across the cobbles in the direction of the raven pens.

Pea wasn't sure if it was the heads on spikes

or the snow, but Tinkerbell was transformed. Pea thought she hadn't looked so excited in weeks. It was like she was back to her old mischievous self.

'What exactly are you up to?' said Clover, nudging her while Mum nipped to the loo.

'Nothing! It's like I said before – I just really like history now.' Tinkerbell grabbed the map, found Tower Green, and pointed through the snow to a grassy spot. 'Anne Boleyn had her head cut off just over . . . there.'

Pea felt her heart skip a beat, then went pale, and had to have a little sit down on a bench. Now she was here, in a real place where a real beheading had happened, it didn't seem thrilling at all.

'Let's save visiting that part for later, shall we?' said Mum.

So Tinkerbell tugged them up to the Bloody Tower, where a mannequin of Walter Raleigh represented his years of imprisonment ('Oh, bum – he was beheaded at Westminster, not here,' she said, reading the guidebook, disappointed), and several rooms were dedicated to telling the tragic tale of the two boy princes, allegedly murdered by Richard III. Then they went down into the dungeons, dark and drippy, with chains dangling from the walls and blood-curdling screams piped from hidden speakers.

Mum decided they could all do with some fresh air, even if it was snowing even harder now.

They huddled in the shelter of an old wall and watched the guardsman outside the so-called Queen's House, who marched up and down every five minutes so the tourists had something to take photos of. Sam One timed him with his watch. Pea found it hard to concentrate: Anne Boleyn had been beheaded just *there*, not 100 metres away – she could picture the smelly peasantish crowds who had come to watch; almost see the glint of sunlight as the axe blade fell . . .

'Can we look at the Crown Jewels now?' she said, shivering.

'Good idea,' said Mum.

They queued and queued, and the Crown Jewels sparkled and glowed under the hot lights of the crammed exhibition room.

They stumbled out into the tumbling snow again, and walked along the top of the walls, watching it fall on the Thames. Pea was very glad they weren't meant to be going swimming in it in a few days – though she still worried about finding an alternative.

'I think I've learned enough about Henry the Eighth now,' croaked Pea, still feeling queasy, though she was keeping her eyes firmly turned away from the beheading spot.

'Me too,' said Sam One, who was wearing three fleeces and a ski jacket, and had gone rather sweaty.

Clover looked plaintively at her watch, her nose bright red from the cold.

Mum sighed. 'I suppose school would be over in a couple of hours anyway . . .'

'Gift shop gift shop gift shop,' said Tinkerbell, grabbing her wrist and pulling.

'Oh, go on then,' Mum said, rolling her eyes.

Gift shops were Mum's weakness. She understood absolutely that fudge with a picture of a castle on it was much more delicious than the kind you could get in the newsagent's for a quarter of the price, and that one could never have too many giant pencils or playing cards or magic rocks.

The Tower shop did not disappoint. There were tapestry cushions with crowns on, china thimbles printed with Henry's fat gingery face, and London buses galore. Pea found a beautiful hand-embroidered Anne Boleyn, which she so wished she could have added to her project: it was a Christmas-tree decoration, with gold twine poking out of Anne's head in a loop, but she planned to like it all year round. Clover picked out delicate silver stud earrings with bejewelled crowns on, which turned out to have real sapphires and rubies on them and were the sort of price you thought must be a typo, so she swapped them for dangly red phone boxes that cost £4. Sam One chose pencils. Mum dithered between a snow globe with Big Ben in it and a fridge magnet of Tower Bridge, and decided to get both, because Vitória could have one as a present. Tinkerbell's choice was a given: she always wanted one of those long bars of milk chocolate with gold print on the wrappers.

Mum pointed the way.

Pea watched Tinkerbell dodge and weave through the crowd towards the chocolaty section. She watched her fingering the bars, weighing two in her hand. She looked away for a moment – just a moment – to help Sam One choose between a lump of quartz and a sheet of stickers for Sam Two, as a group of Spanish schoolchildren, bored and loud, drifted across the aisle, blocking her view.

When they moved away, Tinkerbell was gone.

CHAPTER 12

TINKERBELL

'Do you think we should tell them?' whispered Pea.

Pea, Clover and Sam One had been gently ushered past the NO ENTRY TO THE PUBLIC and PRIVATE signs, through unclipped velvet ropes, into the bowels of the Waterloo Barracks. They now sat on a row of chairs outside a hushed office, amidst piled-up cobwebby old exhibits, listening to Mum sniffle her way through a description of the missing Tinkerbell.

Seven years old. Um, about four feet tall. British Jamaican – black hair, brown eyes. Purple coat, jeans, green wellies with frogs on. No, she doesn't have a phone.

'Tell them what?' said Clover, trying to peep through the crack in the door.

'About the ex-merminating.'

Sam One gave her a blank look.

Clover turned her pale blue eyes on Pea and looked stern and big-sisterly. 'Tink's missing, Pea. That's a bit more urgent than some stupid game she was playing weeks ago.'

Inside, Mum audibly discovered that she did not, after all, carry a photograph of her youngest daughter in her handbag. The door opened, and a man in a suit hurried out to locate a fresh box of tissues.

'But what if she isn't missing?' Pea hissed, waiting till he was gone. 'What if Tink never stopped ex-merminating? What if this is all part of the plan, and she set the whole thing up, and now Mum's in there telling the police and whoever about it when really Tink's gone off somewhere on her own and is totally fine?'

Clover frowned. 'But . . . how would going missing in the Tower of London have anything to do with mermaids?'

Pea bit her lip. It didn't, really.

Inside, an old-fashioned telephone began to ring and ring. Over it, they could hear the tissue-box man trying to say reassuring things about the castle being very large, and children quite often getting lost and coming back right as ninepence (whatever that meant). But all Pea could think about was the dark dripping dungeon with chains on the walls. In amongst the stack of wonky armour and TOILETS signs in the corridor were old information panels, showing the same paintings as the guidebook: the two lonely boy princes, locked up in the dark without even a candle. There was even a stiff plastic mannequin's hand, groping out from behind the panel as if pleading for rescue.

It was too awful to think about. But she did anyway.

Until there was a familiar voice yelling in the corridor, and the sound of someone Britishly mumbling that this was a private area of the castle, and that madam really must vacate the premises at once.

'Shut your face up, sir, I am going in to— Oh, my girls – hey, I been looking all everywhere!'

Vitória barrelled towards them, leaving the mumbler in her wake. She was not her usual impeccable self: the sleek caramel hair was bunched under a scarf, her jeans were shoved into Mum's tall boots, and there was a look of clammy panic on her face.

'I got this for your mum, yeah?' she said, flapping a sheet of paper at them. 'I don't know when it comes – I'm sleeping, I'm putting my feet up, yeah? And then I find this on the mat.'

Mum emerged, even more badgery around the eyes than before, and flopped into Vitória's arms. 'Tinkerbell . . . missing . . . my fault . . .' she whimpered.

'I know!' said Vitória, extricating herself. 'Look, there is a note from like a kidnapper person, yeah?'

Vitória thrust the letter into Mum's hand, but she was shaking too hard to read.

Clover took it from her, and she and Pea pored over it.

It was a classic ransom note, with words spelled out in letters cut from a newspaper (single letters at first, then whole words, as if the kidnapper had got slightly bored towards the end).

I aM A KiDNAppeR
OF TiNKErBELL
GiVe ME £999 PouNDs
AnD 100 bAgs of
HaRIBo
OR I WILLCHOP
HER UP

'Oh my God!' said Clover.

'Haribo?' said Sam One.

'Yeah, I thought that was kind of weirdo peculiar too,' said Vitória. 'And nine hundred and ninety-nine pounds is not very much money really to give back a whole person, right? I mean, that's not normal. In Brazil when people do a kidnap they want some *reals* for their troubles, yeah?'

'That horrible child of mine,' said Mum, half laughing, half furious.

'You mean . . .' said Pea, who had gone beyond picturing Tinkerbell in a hellish dungeon all the way to the tragic-faced police officer on the doorstep bringing the bad news so she could be noble and stoic in the face of despair, and was reluctant to give that up quite yet.

'"I will chop her up" does sound like . . .' said Clover.

'Tinkerbell,' said Vitória. 'So . . . you think Tinkerbell has sort of kidnapped herself?'

'I'll chop her up myself when I get my hands on

247

her!' said Mum, sinking into a chair with a tearful giggle.

'Wait,' said Sam One. 'I don't understand. If Tinkerbell wrote the note, and set it all up . . . then where is she now?'

There was silence. No one had the answer to that. The mystery wasn't over at all. The imaginary tragic policeman might be a real one, because Tinkerbell really *was* missing in the cold and the snow, and suddenly Pea didn't feel at all noble and stoic. She clutched her thumbs, but it didn't help.

'What if—?' she said, wondering if it was too impossible a coincidence to set up a fake kidnapping on the very day you actually did get snatched for real. But Mum had her arm hooked around her neck, holding her tight, and it seemed best not to say it out loud.

Sam One's mobile phone rang. (He had one of his own, which had caused a certain amount of undignified sulking from Clover.) He talked quietly, then held the phone out.

'It's Mum Gen,' he said. 'She wants to talk to you.'

Mum opened her mouth, looked at Sam One, then erupted into sobs again.

Clover patted her shoulder, took the phone, and went into a corner to explain things to Dr Paget.

'She's on her way.'

There was a lot of mumbling and discussion about who should go where, but no one really wanted to go anywhere without Tinkerbell, and they were still arguing when Dr Paget arrived.

She was wearing a hat with bells and reindeers on it, but in all other respects she was calm and sensible and undistracted by the snow. She looped an arm around Sam One, hugged Mum, then went off to be brisk at the police. Then she came back, and sat them all down.

'It seems,' she said gently, 'as if Tinkerbell has run away.'

Mum clutched at another tissue.

'Now, the police think – because of the note,

you see – that she must have been planning it for some time, which is good, because that means she might have left some evidence behind to give us clues: bus timetables, perhaps, or something in the internet history on your computer.'

Pea thought that wasn't likely, since it hadn't been switched on for days, but it wasn't the right time to say so.

'So they'll search in her room?' said Clover, looking anxiously at Pea.

She was thinking of *My First Atlas*, Pea could tell. And the box of *Marinamail!*

'Yes, Clover. But you might be able to save time by having a little think about where she might go. Perhaps a best friend's house?'

Pea bit her lip. No one could come up with one.

'She hasn't really found one in London,' said Clover eventually.

Dr Paget nodded solemnly. 'And favourite places that she likes to go?'

No one could come up with any of those, either.

'So was she not very happy about you all moving here?'

There was an awful silence. Pea looked at the snow falling softly outside the window, and thought about how sad she would have been without her attic, and Zhou (who was her friend at least for an afternoon), and Eloise (because all those lunches had been fun), and Bethany (who wasn't nasty or unkind, and would make a lovely best friend for someone), and Sam One, of course. Tinkerbell hadn't even had those to fill up the time; just lots of plotting to be somewhere else.

Mum made a little whimpery noise which Pea found quite scary, and Dr Paget somehow managed to arrange things so that Vitória took Mum off to find the sugary tea machine.

'What about Christmas?' asked Dr Paget, settling comfortably beside them on the bench.

'Everyone's family does it a little bit differently. What's it like at your home?'

Clover explained about the *pinnekjøtt*, and the Julenissen, and the swimming, and the bacon sandwiches.

'And this year?' prompted Dr Paget.

'Same as always,' said Clover.

'No,' said Pea wretchedly. 'It won't be at all.'

And she explained to Dr Paget about trying to find somewhere for them to go swimming, and emailing Clem, and worrying about whether there was any bacon in the fridge. Then she kept talking. About ex-mermination. About all Tinkerbell's careful plotting. And as she spoke, Pea realized that she and Clover had missed the most obvious thing of all. None of it had been about mermaids, or Marina Cove. It had been about wanting to go home.

Clover's eyes went wide as she realized the same thing.

'She'll have gone back to Tenby,' said Clover

urgently. 'That's home for Tink. That's where Christmas happens. She'll have gone to Tenby to see her dad.'

There was a clack and a splatter. Mum had caught the very end of Clover's words, and dropped a plastic cup of sugary tea all over the polished stone floor.

'But she can't!' Mum cried. 'He's coming here!'

'He is?' said Pea.

'Of course he is! He's coming to stay, so he can bring presents and see Clover's play, and it was meant to be a lovely surprise and— Oh, no. He'll have left already! There'll be no one there!'

Panic broke out.

Dr Paget and Mum ran to tell the police. Pea and Clover were instructed by Vitória to help mop up the sugary tea, which Clover grumbled about but Pea knew was only to give them something to do. Sam One phoned Dr Skidelsky, who was in Edinburgh, just in case she had any suggestions.

The snow went on falling, thicker and thicker.

There was much anxious discussion of ways to get to Tenby. The trains took seven hours from London: Paddington to Swansea, Swansea to Tenby. There wasn't a bus. Even if there had been, no one could think of a way even Tinkerbell could've got her hands on enough money for a ticket, but then it *was* Tinkerbell. *Can she drive?* the suited man asked, which made Mum shout, 'She's SEVEN YEARS OLD!' at him, and that made everyone get upset, because seven was awfully small to be trying to go to Tenby all alone.

Mum's phone rang again. It was Clem. Mum paled and pressed the phone into Dr Paget's hands – and as they spoke, she looked grimmer and grimmer.

'They've closed the Severn Bridge because of the weather, so he drove round the long way, but there's a big jam outside Bristol, and he thinks he might be stuck there for hours.'

Pea shivered.

Mum sank onto the bench, and hugged Clover and Pea to herself, mumbling.

'He says, should he take a train to London, or try to get back to Tenby?'

'I don't know,' whispered Mum, looking imploringly at Dr Paget. 'I don't know. Oh, Tink. What if she *is* on a train? She won't know what to do. Those platforms are freezing. Oh, if only it was after Christmas she'd have a mobile phone – it's wrapped up, under the tree . . .'

Pea wondered if there might be one for her too, and then felt like a terrible human being who probably didn't deserve Christmas presents at all for caring about presents when Tinkerbell was lost in the snow.

She saw Clover checking her watch – less than four hours till the play was due to start – and then she looked stricken with guilt too. Pea gave her a forgiving sort of hug.

Then the suited man came to tell them he'd heard on the radio that most of the train network was now closed, and there were major hold-ups on all the motorways – some of which were now closed too.

Dr Paget was very rude to him. Sam One looked quite taken aback. Dr Paget did too.

'We can take Vitória's car!' said Clover. 'Drive to Bristol and pick Clem up, and then keep going till we get to Tenby. Or come back here.'

Vitória shook her head. 'I sold it.'

'You sold your car?' said Clover, appalled. 'Why would you sell your car?'

Vitória caught Mum's eye, looked tearful, and then snapped at Clover that there were more important things to worry about – which Clover snapped back at, and then Mum shouted at her, and Pea clutched her thumbs so hard they went white, but tears still began to roll down her face.

Dr Paget stepped in and made a plan.

After they'd all driven home, Mum and Dr Paget would go and search every train station on the route, and see if they could find Tinkerbell.

Clem would keep driving towards them, doing the same. Clover and Pea would stay at home, in case Tinkerbell turned up there. Vitória would check on Sam Two, because she had been left alone, possibly vomiting into a washing-up bowl, all this time. They would all phone each other every hour, and more often if need be.

Pea looked at Clover to see if she would mention the play, but she didn't.

Somehow that made it seem very terrible indeed.

They went home by police car (which Tinkerbell would have loved, Pea thought – Oh, thumbs, *thumbs*). Mum flitted hopelessly around the darkened house room by room, just in case Tinkerbell might be sitting in the dark.

Dr Paget popped in to see Sam Two while Vitória made up flasks of coffee. Then Mum squeezed Pea and Clover painfully tight, and went off in a big London cab, just like the one they'd arrived in.

It seemed so long ago now.

Clover lay on her bed, weeping over her furled-up, dog-eared Wicked Queen script.

Vitória made sandwiches and put out the Monopoly board for Pea and Sam One, popping next door every twenty minutes to stick her nose round Sam Two's bedroom door, and gabbling on her phone in Brazilian Portuguese.

The snow went on falling.

Vitória wrapped them all in medicinal duvets and blankets, even though the heating was on and no one was poorly.

Pea had bought a hotel on Fleet Street and two houses on Mayfair and Park Lane when she heard it: quite faint at first, but then quicker and quicker.

The piano, through the wall between the houses.

Chopsticks.

The duet.

Sam One looked at Pea. Vitória wrinkled her

nose. Clover appeared in the doorway, looking very rumpled and red-eyed.

'Who's playing the piano?' she asked.

And they raced next door.

The piano-playing stopped abruptly as they skidded up the gravelly path, and as Vitória put the key in the front door, thumping footsteps could be heard inside.

'Oi!' yelled Vitória, marching over the threshold.

There was a feeble coughing from upstairs.

They all ran up, to find Sam Two lying in her tiny, flowery-wallpapered bedroom with a blanket pulled half over her legs, looking breathless and sweaty.

'Hello?' she said, in a quavery, unwell voice, as if just waking up. 'Did something happen?'

'Shush up, you,' said Vitória. 'Where is she? Where is you, Tinkerbell? And I am not even a little bit joking now, yeah?'

Sam Two looked innocent, and draped a

pale, sickly arm across her forehead to prove it.

There was a scrunchy gravel noise outside, then a knocking at the door.

'Hello? Are you all over here? Why's your front door wide open, girls?'

'Clem!' breathed Clover, rushing out to the stairs as he ran up them, and flinging her arms around him.

'Clem!' said Pea, clutching Vitória's arm.

'Daddy?' said a muffled voice.

It sounded as if it came from inside the walls.

Sam Two went on looking innocent and sickly, but her eyes slid sideways.

'Tink?' said Pea, feeling a little leap of hopefulness. 'Are you really here?'

'Oh, bottoms,' said Sam Two.

There was a scraping noise like a bed being moved next door, then a perfect door-shaped hole swung open in Sam Two's bedroom wallpaper, to reveal Tinkerbell, standing in her own bedroom.

'Am I in trouble?' she whispered.

She was. But Clem said it could be dealt with after he'd hugged her for a week or two, and phoned Mum to let her know Tinkerbell was not a lost icicle in a train station after all. He had to hold the phone away from his ear when he got through, and then pass it to Tinkerbell, who said 'Sorry' and 'Very, very sorry' occasionally, over alternating squeals of joy and shouty noises.

Vitória called the police, and made Tinkerbell say she was 'very, very sorry' to them too.

'So,' said Clem. 'Clover, when does this play of yours start?'

THE FAMILY TREE

The production of *Snow White and the Seven Dwarfs* at Greyhope's that year was universally agreed to be both memorable and festive.

For nearly half the play there were only four dwarfs (the other three had been kept away by snow). Snow White had to double up as the Wicked Queen (*and* her talking reflection), as Eloise was the only one who knew both parts. The Huntsman was played by Mrs Sharma, miming soundlessly, with Bethany shouting the dialogue from a chair at the side of the stage, as she had slipped on an icy pavement that morning and sprained her ankle. The audience was made up almost entirely of Molly's relatives – though luckily she had two rows' worth, and they were very enthusiastic.

By the time Clover, Pea, Tinkerbell, Sams One and Two, Vitória and Clem arrived, Eloise's constant talking to herself was beginning to take its toll. She had accidentally promised the four dwarfs that she would 'do the hoovering and all that sort of thing' in her most Wicked Queenly high-pitched cackle instead of the gentle voice of Snow White, knocked the mirror frame over (it had landed on Bethany's bandaged ankle, causing a ten-minute interval while Mrs Sharma practised her first aid), and was visibly quivering at the prospect of the next scene.

'A comb, for me?' said Snow White softly. 'How kind of you, mysterious old woman!'

Eloise scurried round the cardboard wall of the dwarfs' cottage, pulled on her black Wicked Queen wig, pulled on her grey Wicked-Queen-in-Disguise wig over the top of that, and peered in through the window.

'You are welcome, dear girl,' croaked the Wicked Queen.

Eloise scurried back to the other side of the window, pulling off the wigs.

'Really?' said Snow White.

Eloise put the wigs back on.

'Yes, my dear,' croaked the Wicked Queen.

Eloise pulled the wigs off.

'Thank you, old woman. Will you comb my hair for me, through the window?'

There was a pause as Eloise put the wigs back on, held up the comb, and hesitated.

'Yes, I will!' shouted Clover from the back of the hall.

'Oh, thank God for that,' said Eloise loudly, in a most un-Snow-White-like voice.

Molly's relatives cheered.

There was another brief interval. Behind the scenes, Clover pulled on her magnificent purple floor-length cloak, and though she'd accidentally left all her stick-on warts at home, she looked thoroughly wicked. Vitória, after much hissy whispering in the wings, was persuaded to play the Wicked Queen's reflection. Pea and the Sams were handed spare beards.

'I can't,' hissed Pea. 'I'll get stage fright.'

'Course you can,' said Clover. 'It can't possibly be more scary than everything else that's happened today.' Then she fumbled in her pocket, pulled out a long handwritten note, and cleared her throat.

'Members of the Drama Club,' Clover said grandly, 'I would like to take this opportunity to say—'

Mrs Sharma plucked the note out of her hand.

'But it's my Director's pre-performance pep talk!' protested Clover. 'Every show should start with one!'

But Mrs Sharma said that they seemed to have managed without so far, and the audience was waiting. Clover took a deep breath, nodded, and swept out onto the stage, ready to comb Snow White's hair.

Pea waited in the wings, quite speechless with fear, and trembled as she stepped onto the stage, but luckily the other dwarfs spoke all the lines, so all she had to do was hold an axe and look short. Comfortingly, she could see Clem in the audience, with Tinkerbell sitting right beside him, her hand clasped tightly in his in case she got any ideas.

They got all the way to Snow White lying in the glassy coffin before the hall doors crashed open again, and Mum and Dr Paget came flying through.

'Tinkerbell! Oh, my small, terrible, awful, beloved, wonderful, evil child!' Mum yelled, sweeping her up right in the middle of one of the dwarfs making a very sad speech about not having anyone to do the hoovering any more.

Then Mum kissed Clem on the cheek, and sniffled, and clung to Dr Paget as if she didn't quite want her to stop being in charge, not yet.

Clover shushed her, and Mum meekly sat down.

'Sorry! Sorry!' she hissed, giving Clover a wave,

and then noticing the others up on stage, and waving at them too. 'Gosh, hello, Vitória, she's got you up there too. And my Pea – oh, well done. And Sam! Both of you! Sorry, we're interrupting. Carry on, carry on.'

There was another small delay as a bearded Sam Two was beckoned from the stage, head drooping, because naughty children didn't deserve to be dwarfs. She was to sit on her own at the back (Dr Paget said sternly) and think about all the trouble she'd caused by hiding Tinkerbell.

Then the play carried on, in a glorious riot of missed cues, miming Prince Charmings, missing dwarfs and Brazilian reflections who announced, 'You are, like, totally ugly, innit, missus,' when asked to name the fairest of them all.

As Clover went dancing off the stage in her enchanted shoes, and Molly made fake kissy noises from her chair to accompany Eloise and Mrs Sharma holding hands in the grand finale, the whole audience stood up and applauded – so loudly that a slanted window in the roof popped open under the weight of snow, and thwomped onto Snow White and Prince Charming, covering them completely.

Molly's relatives clapped and cheered even louder.

'Was that meant to happen?' asked Clem, in a whisper.

'Let's say that it was,' Mum whispered back.

There were mince pies for afterwards (supplied by Mrs Sharma, who said she felt that way at least she had contributed something), and everyone stood around admiring beards as snowflakes floated through the open window onto the stage.

Clover sat under it in her purple cloak, letting them fall on her upturned face.

Pea thought she looked like a painting. There was a story in it, at least; one with magical snow that turned to gold and silver and rubies when it landed. She sat next to Clover, to feel the flakes melt on the sticky part of her chin where the beard had been.

'Were we all right?' asked Eloise, hovering before Clover, looking very frayed. 'We didn't think you were coming, so we just sort of had to start without you.'

Pea held her breath. Clover wasn't always especially generous about theatre things.

But Clover stood up and shook Eloise very solemnly by the hand. 'I'm the proudest Director in the whole world,' she said. 'And you all did brilliantly.'

'I don't know how you remembered all those lines,' Pea said to Eloise.

'Headphones,' said Eloise. 'I recorded the whole show, and listened to it over and over till it all went in.'

Clover's eyes lit up, and she hurried away to suggest official Drama Club headphones to Mrs Sharma for their next play.

'I liked your beard,' said Molly.

'Thanks,' said Pea. 'How's your ankle?' she asked as Bethany hobbled over.

They all ate mince pies, and laughed about the things that had gone wrong, and Pea thought that now she wasn't so frantic about one of them being her *best* friend, she might like to get to know all three of them better.

'Top marks, Pea-hen,' said Mum, wrapping her in a warm, fuzzy, jasmine-smelling hug. 'I never thought we'd see you on a stage! You were fantastic.'

'You really were,' said Clem. 'All of you. But now I think it's time to go home.'

Suddenly all the excitement of the day caught up with Pea in a rush, and she found that her feet wouldn't quite go in a straight line.

They took taxis home (one for the Paget-Skidelskys and Vitória, one for the Llewellyns), and Pea was picked up and carried to bed by Clem, only half awake as he did so.

When she woke up the next morning she was still in her clothes, and pillow fluff was stuck to her chin as if she'd never taken off her dwarf's beard.

It turned out to be a whole new sort of Llewellyn Christmas.

Mum locked herself in the study with her manuscript, and was offered small tempting encouragements to get her through the chapters (proper ones that were finished and didn't have ADD EXCITING ARGUMENT SCENE HERE notes halfway through; Pea checked).

250 words = satsuma
500 words = one Quality Street green triangle
1000 words = mince pie
End of chapter = large glass of mulled wine

Clover and Pea sat down with Clem to have a very sensible grown-up talk about ex-mermination, and which parts they should both have told Mum about from the beginning – and which parts Mum probably didn't ever need to know, especially not in the middle of finishing a book.

Then Tinkerbell was made to explain exactly

what she'd been up to. It turned out that the whole scheme had begun with Pea's messages in footballs.

'Only ours were messages under the nailed-up door,' she said. 'Sam Two started posting me notes underneath it, because the other side of it is in her bedroom. Then we got the idea that it would be much better if we didn't have to just write notes to each other. So we unscrewed the door.'

'That's why you needed the screwdriver,' said Pea. 'And why I sometimes couldn't find you.'

'And why sometimes I wouldn't let anyone in,' said Tinkerbell. 'Though one time you and me did play a whole game of Monopoly while Sam Two hid under the bed.'

'Really?' said Pea, impressed. Then she looked at Clem, and remembered how much trouble Tinkerbell had caused. 'I mean, how naughty! We did tell her not to open that door, Clem, I promise.'

Clem smiled understandingly. Then he looked serious again. 'And the kidnapping plan?'

Tinkerbell looked sheepish. 'I didn't think it was a very good idea! But Sam Two said it would be a brilliant way to scare Mum into leaving London. She gave me maps and instructions for how to get the Tube home, and lent me Dr Skidelsky's Oyster card. And I did get all the way back here!' Tinkerbell looked at her hands, and her voice went quiet. 'But it was scarier than I thought it would be, travelling on my own. I got on the wrong platform, and the train went the other way from what I wanted it to. In the snow, everything looks different. I tried going back to the Tower of London, but I couldn't find that either. In the end I got in a black taxi, and Sam Two paid for it out of the coffee jar in their kitchen.'

Clem looked quite peaky. Pea didn't blame him: it was horrible to think how many things could've gone wrong.

'It was Sam Two's idea! And she's older than me, so it's more her fault than mine!' But even

273

Tinkerbell didn't look very convinced by her argument.

Clem very quietly and slowly went through all the things Tinkerbell had done wrong, and all the reasons why she must never, ever, do anything like it again. Then he said that he was very sorry about missing half term, and that he and Mum would make sure to arrange lots of visits from now on, which they would always tell all three of them about.

'You needn't worry about me any more, though,' said Tinkerbell as Sam Two arrived in the kitchen. 'I like living here now. And I'm much too busy with other projects.'

She and Sam Two poked through cupboards.

'Aha!' said Sam Two, holding up a hammer.

Tinkerbell beamed.

Clem took the hammer, wincing, and wouldn't give it back even after Sam Two explained that they were 'only' going to build a toboggan for Wuffly by taking the garden shed apart. Clem found an old tea tray and helped them build a slope out of snow instead. Wuffly, it turned out, was not a fan of slopes, but everyone else liked it.

Clover performed a solo version of her full Wicked Queen role (warts and all) for a select audience of family members who were too polite to say no, plus Wuffly.

Pea hung her Anne Boleyn decoration on the tree.

Tinkerbell was very good, and remembered to keep saying sorry.

Clem stayed until Christmas Eve breakfast (as had been planned all along, apparently), and until then let himself be taken around Queen's Park for twirly pastries several times a day, watching the snow turn from fluff to mush to nothing at all. They still hadn't found anywhere to go swimming, but they all agreed that London in the snow more than made up for it. Clem said he liked London as a place to visit, and wrote down the date of his next trip in his diary, so everyone would know when he was coming to stay.

They piled him up with a bagful of presents, and kissed him goodbye in the hallway.

Clem's were not the only suitcases waiting there for another taxi.

'Vitória, that's your jewellery box,' said Clover, picking up the embroidered case from the top of the pile. 'And your laundry basket. Why are your things here?'

'About that . . .' said Mum, looking upset. 'Oh, I'm sorry, Vitória, I know I promised to tell them earlier – it's just, with everything else that's been going on . . .'

Vitória took them all back into the sun room to explain. It turned out that her mother back in Brazil was getting divorced, and her sister was having a baby, and really she had only come to Britain to be an au pair to improve her English for a few years – so it was time for her to go home.

'It's not anything to be all sad about, yeah? It's just a thing that happens. People go different places, and maybe you don't see them again for a long while, and maybe you don't see them again ever at all, but it was nice when you knew them, right? So you have the nice memories, and if you get sad you think of those, and then it's all right. Yeah?'

'But who will look after us?' said Clover, her hand instinctively straying to the coiling hairdo that Vitória had spent an hour on just that morning.

'Ach, don't worry, your mum will find a new one of me to help her out, no trouble.'

'Will you go off and look after some other family instead of us?' asked Pea.

'Maybe,' said Vitória. 'If I do, I'll send you pictures.'

Tinkerbell stared at Vitória, thinking hard. 'I'm very sorry about the bat in your knickers,' she said eventually.

Clem's eyes widened in horror.

Vitória said she was forgiven, and gave them all a goodbye hug.

Then she handed them each a Christmas

present, wrapped in shiny silver paper, and told them they could open it right away.

Pea's hands shook once she saw what was inside. A 'P' necklace, just like Anne Boleyn's. 'Thank you so, so, so much,' she whispered.

Vitória smiled, and hooked it carefully around her neck.

Clover had a set of underwear: yellow, with matchy pants.

Tinkerbell's was a giant plastic rat. She was overjoyed, and made plans to put it in Sam Two's knicker drawer at once.

Clem jingled his car keys.

The bags were piled into the car, Clem's first, then Vitória's, as her train station was the first stop.

Pea waved so hard her wrist and elbow and shoulder hurt, but she kept waving till the car was completely out of sight.

And then they were gone.

The raspberry-red door closed. It was impossible not to feel flat and sad all of a sudden –

even with all the tinsel round the light switches and the two-metre Colorado Blue Spruce.

'What do we do now?' said Clover.

Then a slow, awkward plinking drifted through the wall.

'That's not Sam Two,' said Tinkerbell. 'She got loads better than that.'

'Do you think Dr Skidelsky's back from Edinburgh?' asked Pea.

'Let's go and find out!' said Mum.

They spent the rest of Christmas Eve at the house next door, watching *A Muppet Christmas Carol* on DVD, which was the Paget-Skidelsky's most important family tradition – one even Dr Skidelsky liked. Pea thought they should adopt that one too; maybe instead of the swimming.

There were chocolate-dipped oranges, and mince pies, and they lingered till it was dark and late, and Mum remembered she still had the last few pages to write before midnight came, and her deadline was past.

'Father Christmas might not come if I miss it,' she said, with a tinkling laugh.

'Really?' whispered Tinkerbell, hanging back behind the others.

'No, don't be silly,' said Pea – though she wasn't at all sure.

Stockings were hung (on the Hannah Montana inflatable sofa, because there wasn't a fireplace).

Goodnight kisses and promises not to get up too early were given.

Then they all went to bed.

Pea lay awake, as she always did on Christmas Eve, and wished she felt sleepy. She looked at her attic beams, and her pinned-up emails, and her shelf-desk with its pile of library books, and she thought that she would always miss Tenby, and she had liked the houseboat in Norway a lot, but that this was definitely her new favourite home. Then she gasped. There was something she'd promised herself to remember, and it was quite impossible to think of sleeping till it was done.

She hopped out of bed and hurried over to her desk. Then she tiptoed through the darkness down the stairs, across the kitchen, and out into the garden. She slipped the note she'd scribbled inside the old red-and-blue football that lay on the muddy grass, and threw it, as high as she could, over the fence.

Task done, she tiptoed back into the hall – and heard the sound of tapping keys. There was a light still on under the study door.

She turned the handle very carefully, and found Mum sitting in the lamplight, her eyes sparkling, face lit up with the glow from the computer screen. She tapped the keys quickly – one, two, three. Then she turned to Pea, and gave her a dazzling secretive smile.

'Guess what?' she whispered.

'What?' said Pea.

'I've finished my book.' Mum nodded at the clock. 'Just in time.'

It was five minutes to midnight.

'Off to bed, sleepy head,' she said.

'Nighty-nighty-night,' said Pea.

In the morning, the Llewellyn house was filled with the smell of bacon sandwiches. The stockings on the Hannah Montana sofa were fat and lumpy. On the two-metre Colorado Blue Spruce hung the papery, hand-drawn decorations: Clover, Pea and Tinkerbell, Wuffly, Mum and Marina Cove, Vitória and Clem, all waiting for Christmas to begin.

Dear Sam,
Thank you for being my friend. Happy Christmas!
Pea xxx